GHOULS OF THE UNDERCITY

Richardson had several guided tours that he alternated throughout the week. His favourite was a trip around the Old City, visiting several of the locations where over the years, apparitions had, allegedly, been seen. He would then lead his group into the tunnels and the catacombs beneath street level—into the so-called Undercity; a labyrinthine warren of vaulted, coarse-brick, underground chambers that dated back hundreds of years. In this dark subterranean environment, the poor had lived a squalid, cramped and disease-ridden existence, shut off from the world above. There were countless tales of bloodcurdling horror attached to this place; ones that he would relate and embellish with his own sense of macabre flair... But was it all fiction...?

WILDSIDE PRESS BOOKS BY EDMUND GLASBY

The Ash Murders
The Chaos of Chung-Fu
The Dyrysgol Horror and Other Weird Tales
Ghouls of the Undercity
Labyrinth of The Lost
The Weird Shadow Over Morecambe

GHOULS OF THE UNDERCITY

Tales of the Supernatural

EDMUND GLASBY

WILDSIDE PRESS

TO THE MEMORY OF MY MOTHER

Published by Wildside Press LLC.
www.wildsidebooks.com

CONTENTS

GHOULS OF THE UNDERCITY. 7

MASK OF THE OLMEC 31

THE CONTRACT. 55

THE SONS OF SET-PERIBSEN 77

THE HORROR AT THURLBURY MANOR 109

ABOUT THE AUTHOR. 131

GHOULS OF THE UNDERCITY

Things other than flesh
crawled in the darkness...

David Richardson sat in front of the small mirror applying the final touches to his skull-faced makeup; the chalk-white powder and the dark eye shadow. He grinned, appraising his teeth, which he had already blackened, wondering whether or not to enhance his ghoulish appearance with a little fake blood. After a moment's indecision he chose not to, after all he had gone out in his blood-sucking vampire costume the night before and it was just possible that there would be some who had attended that tour there tonight. It wouldn't do to make his little business—providing 'ghost tours' around the city—look cheap for there were now other tour operators working out there and competition was relatively fierce. It really was a question of showmanship and originality and to that end he wouldn't settle for second best; aspiring to give his customers the most insightful and frightful experience that he could.

In this endeavour Richardson had two main advantages over his competitors. First—he possessed a theatrical background, both in acting and in makeup and costume-design, having worked for over twenty years on some of the, admittedly low-scale, productions that several playhouses in the city had put on. Secondly—he knew much of the ghostly lore pertaining to the city, including the knowledge of the dark, eerie and atmospheric places to visit. When he had started the business, in 1980, he had spent hours trawling the records in the library for the gems that added lustre to the facts that the other guides re-hashed time and time again. On occasion he had, surreptitiously, joined some of the other, inferior—in his view at least—tours, making mental notes and learning one or two things; little tricks of the trade, so to speak. To his satisfaction, there wasn't much that he didn't already know, and plenty of mistakes. The only drawback he faced was the fact that he was a sole operator, a one-man show and, consequently, unlike some of the other tours he had been on he had no paid stooges ready to jump out of the shadows at opportune moments. However this was something he was rather pleased about, preferring a much classier approach.

Richardson had three different tours that he alternated throughout the week, each of approximately one and a half hours duration. By far his favourite and the one he would be leading this evening was a trip around the Old City, visiting several of the locations where over the years, apparitions had, allegedly, been seen. He would then lead his group into the tunnels and the catacombs beneath street level—into the so-called Undercity; a labyrinthine warren of vaulted, coarse-brick, underground chambers that dated back hundreds of years. In this dismal, unlit, subterranean environment unknown numbers of the poor had lived a squalid, cramped and disease-ridden existence, shut off from the world above. There were countless tales of bloodcurdling horror attached to this place; ones that he would relate and embellish with his own sense of macabre flair.

Consulting his wristwatch, Richardson realised he would soon have to set off for the rendezvous point just outside the cathedral—an interesting building in its own right and one into which he used to take tourists until the bishop had learnt about it and brought such activities to a halt. All of his tours began at eight o'clock, regardless of the weather and if the past few nights were anything to go by there would hopefully be a substantial number waiting. It had never ceased to amaze him how much people enjoyed hearing about such horrible facts and ghoulish happenings; eager to learn more about the darker side of the city's history. For evil had happened here. This was undeniable—the evidence and the truth lay buried under the streets, in the cemeteries, in the dark cobbled alleyways and boarded-up houses.

Yet, in spite of all that he knew, Richardson himself was an ardent sceptic. Certainly, many terrible things had happened here; murder, grave-robbing, devil worship and the like but he didn't believe in ghosts. After all, if anyone should have seen one then surely it would have been him after two years intentionally visiting the places they were rumoured to haunt. But the truth of the matter was he had seen and experienced nothing that couldn't be explained in a logical manner.

That said, there had been numerous occasions when some on his tour—individuals claiming to be psychic or some such nonsense—had reported seeing things or having experienced something unsettling. Such 'experiences' included the sighting of an apparition of a young boy down in the Undercity crying in torment, the image of a shadowy Jack the Ripper figure close to where some of the most sadistic and gruesome murders had occurred and the sensation of icy, spectral hands closing around someone's throat. His tours were advertised as being not for the faint of heart and, to date, there had been over a dozen instances when individuals had steadfastly refused to go any further, nine cases of the hysterics, three faintings and one heart attack victim who, thankfully, had been resuscitated by an off-duty doctor who had also been on the tour at the time in question.

Satisfied with his cadaverous visage, Richardson rose from his chair and moved to where a range of mannequin heads sporting various fright wigs rested on a shelf. Tonight he opted for a straggly, grey, shoulder-length hairpiece, which he believed would augment his ghastly facial cosmetics. He put it on and ran his hands through it, raking it with his fingers into even wilder tangles. To complete his look he went to his wardrobe and took out a black cloak with red lining which he fastened around his neck and then grabbed his top hat, his silver wolf-headed cane and his black valise. Inside the case he had a powerful torch, some spare batteries, a wad of information flyers that he would distribute after the tour, a thick bunch of keys enabling him to enter the Undercity, the cemetery and several of the abandoned houses that were of interest and a small, basic first-aid kit in case of minor accidents, mostly as a result of people tripping or banging their heads in the shadowy tunnels into which they would be going.

After checking that everything was in order, Richardson switched off the lights in his changing room and left his small office, exiting onto the street. It was dark and cold and there was a light drizzle in the air. Whistling jauntily, he made for the cathedral.

* * * *

"Dare you venture inside the dark and terror-filled Under-city, where hundreds lived in squalor and poverty? Join me on a journey into a shadow-filled world of horror and crime, where cannibalism was rife and Satan Himself is said to have been summoned. Discover, at first-hand, the dark alleyways where Charles Butterworth, 'The Laughing Ghoul,' stalked and murdered his victims in such a grisly and depraved fashion and learn just why the house at 333 East Street has such a sinister reputation, remaining closed all these years." Richardson spoke eloquently, trying to tout for business among the passers-by for he had been sorely disappointed when, upon arriving at the cathedral, there had been only a middle-aged couple waiting, who had enthusiastically introduced themselves as Lester and Mary Cunningham, American tourists from Boston. A poor showing by any standard. Still, there remained a few more minutes to try and whip up some interest and, as this was a weekend night, there were a lot of people about. "I alone have the key which will enable us to enter." He spotted a tall, elderly, bespectacled man regarding him with measured interest. "You sir, you have the look of someone who is unafraid of the darker side of life and who would be willing to venture into the hellish depths in order to come face-to-face with the living dead, to hear of the stories of mayhem and murder which have left their gruesome stain on this fair—or should I say *foul*—city."

"Well, I think you may have just piqued my interest." The man stepped closer. "Yes, why not. I'll give it a go." Noticing the advertising placard next to Richardson, he dug into his pocket and handed over the admission fee.

"Thank you." Richardson put the money into his wallet. "I can guarantee your enjoyment. Now if you'll just wait a few minutes over here—"

"Hurry up, Stanley. Oh, thank God we haven't missed it." A large, forceful woman pushed her way through the passing crowd, practically hauling a small, bald-headed, bearded man. "We heard about if from some guests staying at our hotel the other evening who told us how much they enjoyed it. This is our last night in the city and we didn't want to miss out, now did we, Stanley?" She threw a disparaging look at her husband. "Well hurry it up, Stanley. Pay the man."

With something of a pathetic, long-suffering look at Richardson, Stanley counted out the required money and paid up.

It was now only two minutes to eight o'clock and Richardson was preparing to start when a group of young men, four in total, turned up. At first, he was concerned, having dealt with brash and offensive types before, who either deliberately sought to ridicule his tours or else proved downright difficult with their disruptive antics. However this group of lads seemed to be relatively well-behaved. Besides, it was slim pickings this evening and he didn't want to turn away four paying customers. News like that would soon get around and the last thing he needed was negative advertising.

"Well, if we're all ready, let us begin. Please, follow me. I'm a fast walker and we've got much to see so do try to keep up." With those words, Richardson set out, his group of nine close on his heels.

Striding purposefully to the side-street at the rear of the cathedral, Richardson led his party away from the main thoroughfares of the city which were now beginning to throng with crowds of weekend evening revellers. Their shouts and laughs faded altogether after a few minutes, the only sounds now audible that of the clatter of shoes on the pavement and the occasional snippet of hushed conversation. Even the group of young men were surprisingly quiet.

They were now entering an area devoid of street lighting and the crumbling houses that loomed high on either side were dark and foreboding, partially decaying structures that no doubt housed countless undesirables. The street before them narrowed further and now Richardson had to use his torch to light the way, informing everyone to stay close and to mind their step. About halfway along, he stopped, shone his torch down a downward sloping passageway that branched off from the street they were on. It was terribly dark along that cobbled lane and, even he had to admit, it was spooky.

"We now stand at the turning to Hobbs Alley—one of the oldest, and some would say, most haunted parts of the Old City. For those of you who don't know, the city you see today has been occupied for well over a thousand years. Now obviously there are only a few small traces of occupation going back as far as that, however much of the present-day buildings are in fact built atop much older structures, some dating back two, three and even four hundred years. The oldest building in the city that still stands is probably the Three Goats Heads public house which dates back to the early Twelfth Century."

"Can we go there and visit the spirits behind the bar?" quipped one of the young men, his comment winning a few laughs from his mates.

Richardson took it all in his stride. "Not on this tour, although that is one of the tours I run and there are some very interesting and unnerving tales to be told about that place. Its name, for instance, comes from a certain Black Magic rite, which utilised said goats' heads, but I digress. Hobbs Alley is infamous for many things but perhaps its greatest notoriety derives from the fact that it was down there, on the twenty-seventh of February 1886 that the mutilated body of a young serving girl, Jayne Wheatley, was discovered. Three days later, a second victim, Rosie Travis, was also found. Then a third, Margaret Brent, again three days later, was found; brutally murdered, torn almost to pieces in an act of unspeakable violence."

"Was that like Jack the Ripper?" asked Mary.

"Hell, Mary, that was in London. Remember we went on that tour last year," replied Lester.

"Although there was some resemblance to the Ripper murders, this was the handiwork of a despicable being some would consider far worse, despite the fact that not so many have heard of him. I'm talking about Charles Butterworth—*The Laughing Ghoul*. I see by the looks on your faces that none of you are familiar with the name—a name that history has, to a large extent, chosen to forget, so wicked were his crimes."

"Either that or you've just made him up," remarked Stanley's wife.

"Why, not at all." Richardson enjoyed it when others challenged his knowledge of the details. "At the end of our little expedition I have certain pamphlets which I will distribute that provide all the information regarding this evening's tour. You'll be able to do some research of your own if you doubt any of what I say."

"Why was Butterworth called The Laughing Ghoul?" asked the elderly gentleman.

Richardson turned. "A good question but the answer will have to wait until later when all will be made clear. Well, if we are ready, we'll head down to where young Jayne Wheatley met her terrible, tragic end. Follow me and—"

"We're not going down there, are we?" asked Mary nervously.

"But of course. I assure you I'll keep the torch on at all times, however the ground is uneven so please take care."

As a tightly-huddled group they went down, the alley narrowing the further they went. There was a cloying, unpleasant smell in the air and it was deathly quiet, claustrophobic, the atmosphere and the knowledge of what may have happened here playing on the nerves of all bar Richardson. After all for him this was familiar territory. He came down this alley with groups twice, sometimes three times a week.

Shadows shrank and crept back again as the guide swung his torch around the walls before directing the beam to the ground at his feet. "It was here, in this godforsaken place that the body of Jayne Wheatley was found—well what was left of her at any rate. You see, when they found her she had been partially consumed. The flesh from her legs, torso and arms had been—"

"Hey, steady on. That's quite enough of that." Lester shook his head with distaste. "I thought we'd come to hear about some good old-fashioned British ghosts not this kind of stuff."

"Well I'm sorry if I've offended you, but I normally only tone down my commentary if there are any children present. Although, that said, more often than not it is they who want to hear all of the gory details. Bloodthirsty little tykes that they are. However, I'll take on board what you say."

A couple of the young men moaned at this, believing it a needless acquiescence on their guide's part. They weren't squeamish and wanted to hear it—guts and all.

"As I was saying, it was here that Charles Butterworth claimed his first victim. The other two were found close by. Butterworth's involvement was only discovered later and indeed only by pure chance, when human remains were found in his house—333 East Street. And it is there that we're going next. Now before we go I normally just ask everyone to stand still and try to mentally picture the scene as it would have been almost a century ago on that dark, terrible night." Richardson deliberately covered the torch with his hand, dimming the light and making the alley even more horrifying.

Shadows seemed to seep and press in towards them as though possessed of their own malign intent. A preternatural, unnerving silence fell, descending upon them like a funeral shroud. It was bordering on the unbearable for some—the two women and Stanley in particular. It was a horrible atmosphere, whether one believed in the bloody murders or not. Varying levels of fear crept into the hearts of all but Richardson as the imagination conjured up ghastly images.

Two agonising minutes passed before Richardson raised his torch. "Well…did anyone experience anything? On previous tours I've had people tell me that they've felt suddenly cold or even heard hideous laughter. On one or two occasions I've had people who claimed to have seen the ghost of Jayne Wheatley or even the phantom of Butterworth himself dressed very much in the same manner as I am."

"I did feel a chill," spoke up Stanley's wife. "A creepy kind of shiver. It was most unpleasant."

"It's an eerie place, I'll say that for it," said the elderly man. "Do people still live in these houses?"

"I don't know," Richardson answered. "I've never seen any lights on behind any of the windows but I assume they do."

"Can we be going now?" inquired Stanley's wife. "I don't like it here."

"I think it's giving her the willies," commented Lester cheekily. His comment received a dark glower from the woman in question but got a few chuckles from the young men.

"Indeed. Follow me." His torch illuminating the way, Richardson took them further into the warren of dingy backstreets.

They went down narrow, uneven flights of stairs and up sloping inclines. At one point they exited onto a relatively major road and the sight of cars and lampposts provided some with a well-needed respite in what was proving to be a most unsettling experience. But then the modern street was behind them and they were once more back in the twisting, cobbled streets and alleys of the Old City.

A malodorous, fetid stench struck at their nostrils.

"Say, what's that God awful stink? Don't you people have working drains?" Lester's nose wrinkled in disgust.

"That, my friend, is the accumulated waste of several centuries," answered Richardson. "You see there were no latrines or sewers back in the days these houses were built and sanitation was virtually non-existent. Much of the effluent was merely tipped from windows where it would fester for weeks. Liquid waste would run down the street, leeching into the very brickwork—hence the better property, if one could say that given the conditions, was always at the top of the hill. The council have not yet tackled this area of the city as it is virtually uninhabited. Indeed, if they finally get round to modernising it I fear we will be losing a piece of history."

The buildings around them were even more dilapidated than those they had already seen with smashed windows and broken doorways. Some bore the scars of past fires and a sense of wickedness seemed to hang over them as though, over the years, they had borne silent witness to acts of great inhumanity. Over to their right, away from some boarded-up houses, which leaned like dying men against one another for support, was a burnt-out church-like building. Once a gathering point for the denizens of this area, now it lay desolate and heavily vandalised, its remaining walls and rafters broken and blackened. This area seemed almost detached from all that was sane and modern and it was doubtful that even daylight would improve the look of the place. At night, with a chill drizzle falling from the dark heavens and a gloomy, spectral mist now beginning to fall and with a character like Richardson, dressed as he was, it bordered on the nightmarish.

"And here we are, East Street. The house we have arrived at is number 333." Richardson shone his torch at a dark, padlocked wooden door set in a stretch of very old wall, the stonework coarse and crumbling. "It is here, within this very house of horrors that Charles Butterworth, the evil perpetrator of those heinous murders, lived; murders that went beyond madness and evil. Behind this door is the house of a truly depraved individual. What terrible sights the police must have witnessed when they entered we can only imagine but if the records are anything to go by then we can but speculate on the gut-wrenching horrors within." Removing his set of keys from his case, he quickly found the one he needed, inserted it into the lock, turned it and opened the door.

By the light from the torch the gathered group could see that the space beyond was a small, bare room.

"Please be careful once inside as there are numerous loose beams and, as you can see, it is rather low-ceilinged, so please mind your head." With that warning, Richardson entered. He waited until everyone was inside before closing the door.

A faint charnel smell hung in the air.

"Charles Butterworth was more than a killer. When the police came here on a tip-off they found far more than they had bargained for. The ground floor was fairly normal—obviously there is no furniture remaining from that time—but it is what they discovered upstairs..." Once everyone was inside, he led them along a shadow-filled corridor, showing them around several fairly nondescript ground floor rooms. They gathered in what had once been the kitchen.

"It sure is a creepy place this," commented Mary.

Lester put his arm around his wife. "I don't know; some nice wallpaper, fitted lights and some pot plants...I reckon—"

There came a loud creak from upstairs as though someone had stepped on a loose board. It came again and was then followed by the sound of a door closing.

"What the hell was that?" cried out several voices at once.

All was quiet.

Richardson swiftly panned the torch around. It was possible that there was someone else in the house with them although that seemed highly unlikely considering the fact that he had had to unlock the property in order to gain access. A vagrant, possibly? On a few occasions he had encountered drunks and homeless individuals down in the Undercity—those unfortunates who had nowhere else to go.

As a group they remained silent for a further thirty seconds.

"Maybe it's the ghost of Charles Butterworth," said Richardson. "Shall we go and see?" There was a slight apprehension in his tone. Realising this, he forced calmness back into his voice. After all, this was but an old, dark house—admittedly it had been the house of a psychopathic, cannibalistic murderer—but a house, nonetheless. To the others, however, the place was genuinely creepy. In the torchlight the imagination was free to run rampant and unchecked and for some—those perhaps more susceptible to the multitude of fears that came crowding in, ringing them around, notably the two women and Stanley—the pressure was becoming unendurable. It was as though some powerful, malevolent presence now lurked here; an evil that was just waiting, readying itself for the best moment at which to reveal itself.

In single file, with the guide in the lead, they started up the stairs. There was a small landing halfway up and there was no banister, making it relatively hard going, more so in the cramped conditions and dim light. There was some disgruntled muttering in addition to a few curses from the young men as they tripped, their ascent almost in complete darkness for they were at the rear of the group. Even with the background kerfuffle, Richardson strained his senses; attempting to hear anything out of the ordinary. He thought he detected a further groan from the floorboards in the room at the end of the corridor indicative of someone—ur something—moving around in there but he wasn't certain. They had all heard a sound when they had been downstairs in the kitchen but he knew from past experience of being in these old buildings how sounds could be deceptive. A gust of wind down an old chimney, the scampering of rats or even the very settling of the building itself due to hundreds of years of age and decay could create a myriad of noises. Noises that those who had been 'conditioned,' as it were, to believe in ghosts, would instantly attribute to the paranormal to the detriment of the mundane.

Gently, Richardson pushed open the door on his right. It was an unfurnished bedroom—rather that is what it had once been. Similarly with the room on his left. He shone the torch inside both permitting the others a brief look. For some reason and despite his rational thinking he was beginning to feel tiny trickles of cold sweat crawling down his back. He had felt like this on one or two previous occasions—more so when there had only been two or three in his group and that 'safety in numbers' feeling of security had seemed virtually non-existent. For perhaps only the second time on one of his 'ghost tours' he longed for a light switch he could just reach out for and click, instantly bathing his surroundings in bright, welcome illumination.

"Just what is it that's beyond this other door?" asked Lester. "Are we going to see a ghost or what?"

Richardson turned, one hand on the door handle. "I make no promises that we'll see any ghosts. Indeed, I, myself, don't believe in them. However, if they do exist then surely it would be in a place such as this. Over the years there have been several investigations by specialists in the field—ghost-hunters or parapsychologists—experts, who, allegedly, have witnessed and experienced dreadful and inexplicable things in the room beyond this door."

"What kind of things?" asked Stanley's wife, her fleshy face shrouded in shadow.

"I believe they took several photographs," answered Richardson. "In some there were—unexplained shapes—things that weren't there at the time the photos were taken; blurred outlines of a man dressed similarly to the reported sightings of Butterworth. There were other things too. Things I'll explain once we're all inside. I should warn you that on previous tours I've had people feel suddenly sick and disorientated upon seeing what lies beyond." When this precautionary statement got no immediate response, he pushed open the door and raised his torch beam.

A grotesque, corpse-like face grinned back at him!

It was almost as though the torchlight had struck a mirror, reflecting back his own hideous, made-up image. However this was a wall painting, daubed onto the coarse brick in garish reds and yellows. The painting was both surreal and unnerving and was clearly the product of an insane mind. The mouth hung wide and stretched; the eyes huge and staring. And as the group moved in they saw that there were many such murals—some mere caricature-like sketches others full-blown works of devilish artistry. All depicted that grinning, triumphant, ugly visage. No matter which stretch of wall one looked at there was a face, the eyes glaring out with a malevolent intensity. Within the confines of the room it gave the viewer the impression that they were caged; and that it was *they* who were the subject of diabolical scrutiny.

Thankfully, at least as far as Richardson was concerned, the room was empty. There was no vagrant lying huddled in newspapers and with a bottle of cheap rotgut close at hand. Such an encounter could have proven awkward and extremely embarrassing. Tourists eager to learn of the city's dangerous and squalid past were seldom as keen to confront these elements of its squalid present.

"Good God!" exclaimed Lester. "Those faces! I take it that's Butterworth?"

"None other. Hence 'The Laughing Ghoul.' It was in this room that he was said to have practised his unholy ceremonies. One rumour has it that it was within this very room that he summoned forth the Devil and that it was this experience which drove him completely insane, making him paint all of these warped self-portraits. Another rumour says that when he called forth Satan, the Devil forced him into painting one face for each person he had murdered. Ah, but I notice your confusion—Butterworth only killed three times, you say. Alas no, you see when the police conducted a search of the house they discovered more bodies—or rather parts thereof. Where? I hear you ask." Richardson pointed the torch beam to the floor. "Why under the very floorboards upon which you now stand. Over twenty-five individuals, or so it is claimed, lay underneath." He grinned upon noticing the shock and revulsion that flickered over some of the other's faces. In a perverse way he loved this little revelation. It never ceased to get a reaction.

Some looked down as though half-expecting putrefying, clawed hands to burst through the floor or to see withered, rotten faces gazing up through gaps in the boards.

"You're kidding, right?" asked Lester, his arm around his wife's shoulder, providing comfort for it was clear that she was feeling uneasy.

Richardson shook his head. "I'm afraid not. It was here, in this diabolical shrine that many unspeakable atrocities were carried out. It is now well-accepted that Butterworth was a leading Satanist and I'm sure he was not working alone. A cabal of devil-worshippers operated from this house, preying on the poor and the vulnerable, obtaining many of their recruits and their sacrificial victims from the surrounding slums and the Undercity, where we shall be going next. There used to be—" he was interrupted by the unsavoury sound of the American woman vomiting.

"Are you okay, honey? I think it's time we got out and got some fresh air," said Lester.

"I agree." With hasty strides, Richardson led them back along the corridor, down the stairs and outside. Here they all gathered, the two women looking pale and sickly in the poor light, their respective spouses trying to comfort them.

"Hey, Mister tour leader."

Richardson turned to face one of the young men, an acne-faced youth in his late teens. "Yes?"

"Well I've just noticed that the old geezer, you know, the guy with the glasses…well, he's missing."

* * * *

A quarter of an hour later, after having re-entered Charles Butterworth's house and conducted a thorough search within, Richardson found himself perplexed and at a loss for answers regarding the man's disappearance. The appropriate thing to do was to call the tour off and inform the police but when he had raised that as a course of action, both Americans and Stanley's wife had volubly stated that they wanted it to continue; a decision given some strength when one of the young men revealed that he had overheard the old man mentioning that he had seen enough. It could be, therefore, that he had just decided to make off without announcing his intent, in which case, assuming that he could find his way back in the dark safely there was no cause for alarm. Such things had happened on the other tours—indeed, now he came to think about it, it was rare that he finished a tour with the same number he had started out with.

"Well, are we going to see this Undercity or whatever it's called?" ventured Lester. "Or are we going to get a full refund?"

"Yes, I, or rather we, came along specifically to see the Undercity, didn't we Stanley?" Stanley's wife pulled her expensive coat tight over her pendulous bulk. "We've heard it's a must see. A once in a lifetime experience."

Richardson was still mentally debating what he should do. It went without saying that the Undercity was the highlight of the tour and it would reflect badly on him if he were to cancel things now. He reached a decision, hoping that he was right about the old man having just opted to abandon the tour and make his own way back. "Very well," he said. "On with the tour. We shall leave the maleficent Charles Butterworth behind and set out for the Undercity—a vast, sprawling underground labyrinth of tunnels and vaults wherein whole generations lived and died." He felt somewhat better now that he had reached a firm decision, assured that he had at least gone back into the house, where the old man had last been seen, in an attempt to locate him. Case and cane in one hand, torch in the other, he marched off, confident in the knowledge that the others would follow.

They soon entered a further maze of narrow, deserted streets. The age-old houses crammed in around them oppressively and with each step that horrendous stench grew.

"In times past, this part of the Old City was often referred to as the 'Necropolis,' which if we have any Classical scholars amongst us will know means 'city of the dead.' Although this area was never used as an actual burial site, at least not to my knowledge, there's little doubt that hundreds, maybe thousands, died in these dismal hovels. Many perished due to malnutrition and disease. Others fell victim to the likes of Butterworth and his cronies. There were also many fires in this area, although none as severe as the blaze of 1826 when almost a third of the Old City was affected. Many of the buildings we can see around us bear traces of that terrible conflagration. However, it was in the Undercity itself where one of the most calamitous fires erupted, killing scores of unfortunates. It must've been a truly terrifying experience; trapped underground, the flames and the smoke, the screams as entire families were burnt to death, unable to escape."

Far away could be heard the faint sound of a police car siren—an incongruous sound considering their surroundings and a small, yet welcome reminder that they hadn't completely stepped outside the modern world. It was difficult to perceive the fact that they were in a city within a city; a frightening, ghastly enclave that lurked within the boundaries of an otherwise relatively sane conurbation filled with schools, hospitals and libraries.

Down a twisting street Richardson led them. On their right loomed a wall some thirty feet in height, its surface cracked and covered in obscene scrawls of graffiti suggesting that local street gangs had at one time frequented this area. Amidst the doodles and the gibberish, one slogan proclaimed '*Charles Butterworth will rise again!*'; the message painted onto the wall in thick, red, sloppy brushstrokes.

"There are a few entrances to the Undercity," announced Richardson, opening his case and removing his set of keys. It was only now that the others realised that there was a cunningly concealed door in front of him. "With several more being found each year. Most are but tunnels, little more than sewer entrances. This one, however, was perhaps the most commonly used by those who either chose or were forced to dwell therein." He unlocked the door and pushed it open.

The stench that assaulted their nostrils was foul; an age-old smell mixed with the hint of sewage, as though a long-closed manhole lid had just been raised. Beyond the door was a stretch of tunnel at the end of which, just visible in the torchlight, could be seen another door.

Once everyone was inside, Richardson closed the door behind them. He then went to the front of the group and led them down the passageway. It was dank and low-ceilinged, the walls curved slightly as though it was a sewer tunnel. The door he was approaching was far older in appearance, with a square metal grille set at head height. With a different key, he unlocked it, the torchlight revealing a flight of stone steps descending into a murky darkness. Water could be heard dripping from somewhere, the steady sounds echoing off the walls.

"Please be careful on the steps." Deeper and deeper Richardson led them down the sloping passages, through tunnels that rang with the muffling echoes of their feet and oozed a thick, viscid moisture from the walls until none but he was sure of the way back. Eventually they left the sewer system and exited, via another downward sloping passage, into a rat-run of interconnected vaulted chambers. Some were sealed off with portcullis-type gates and all were ancient.

There was an air of menace about these subterranean spaces; an aura of evil and cruelty that was almost tangible. In this place of darkness and death only the shadows seemed alive.

"All sorts of ghostly things have been seen down here. Not surprising, I guess, when one considers the grisly history which has literally seeped into the very walls." Richardson continued with his spiel: "In 1779 the crown ordered a violent, merciless assault on the inhabitants in an attempt to clamp down on the rampant lawlessness that, like a contagion, spread from here. Hundreds were butchered in their sleep or rounded up and dragged to the surface where they were either imprisoned or executed. Six years later it was the turn of the church. By order of the bishop the known entrances were sealed off, resulting in mass starvation."

"I didn't think it would be so big," commented Lester, eyes wide as he stared all around.

"This is but one part of the Undercity. Exactly how far it stretches no one actually knows however there are points of access in Grey Chapel Cemetery, Kirkwall Street, St. Cuthbert's Causeway and West Tower Road in addition to the one we entered by. It is said that there may also be entrances near the castle as well as one in the vaults of the cathedral where we started. At the height of its inhabitation it has been suggested that up to six thousand people may have lived down here. It must have been a very basic existence; food and fresh water being scarce and having to be scavenged from above. Sadly, it is a documented fact that cannibalism was rife and there are reports of folk being snatched from above and dragged down here for such a purpose."

"I did a history lesson about Sawney Bean, the Scottish cannibal who lived on the Ayrshire coast," spoke up one of the young men. "He lived in a cave and ate people."

"Ayrshire is a little outside my beat but I can't say that I've heard of him," replied Richardson. "Anyway, if anyone has any questions I'll be pleased to answer them."

Lester ran a hand down the wall, feeling the dampness on the rough surface. "You said earlier that these tunnels were several hundred years old. Well, I've been to Egypt and I've been inside some of the ancient tombs in the Valley of the Kings and I've got to say this place looks a damn sight older even though those tombs were thousands of years old."

"The main part of the Undercity is three hundred, maybe four hundred years old. It could be that there are older parts as yet undiscovered but I doubt it," Richardson replied, casting a casual glance at his watch. It was a quarter past nine; time to be winding things up. "If you're all ready we'll start heading out. I'll be leading you out a different—" He stopped as everything went several shades gloomier and then suddenly dark, the light from his powerful torch dying before going out.

There were a few startled cries.

"Please be calm," Richardson called out. "The batteries on my torch must've died. Just a moment. I've got spares in my—"

"What the hell was that?" Lester called out.

"Something just moved past me," cried one of the young men.

"Oh my God! Oh my God!" screamed Stanley's wife hysterically.

What followed was pure pandemonium. It seemed that everyone was screaming now as panic broke out. In the utter darkness people were floundering and tripping, colliding with others and stumbling, blindly, into the walls as the darkness become peopled by nightmares.

Richardson was fumbling desperately for his spare batteries. He slid one into place and then someone staggered into him, knocking the second battery from his trembling fingers. With a curse, he dropped to his knees and began feeling around hoping that it had not rolled far or down a crack in the floor. It would be pure hell trying to get these frightened people out in pitch darkness.

"Jesus Christ! Something's got a hold of my—" Lester's words were cut short as there came a scratching, ripping sound followed by an obscene, terrible gargling.

Yells and cries reverberated off the Undercity walls, chasing themselves in fading echoes down the age-old tunnels. In the terror-filled darkness it was clear that some had tried to flee from the ensuing madness for their screams now sounded further away. Someone nearby was whimpering, their pathetic mumbled words half-prayer, half-nonsense.

Like a blind man feeling his way forward, Richardson's fingers clamped around the missing battery. He slid it into place and…what he saw as the torchlight illuminated his surroundings once more caused his heart to leap and his stomach to lurch.

Crouched over the bloody, savaged corpse of Lester was a small, naked, thoroughly grotesque being, its skin pale, almost bone-white. The emaciated thing's face was wrinkled and sallow, its eyes huge and black, doll-like. Fresh blood dribbled out of its crooked, tooth-filled maw from where it had been feasting on its victim's torn throat.

Mercifully, Richardson only saw it for a second or two for it recoiled instantly from the bright light, hissing its wrath and shielding its eyes before scampering rapidly away. It vanished almost as quickly as it had appeared, its movements loping and almost spider-like as it clambered up one of the tunnel walls and disappeared into a crack in the ceiling. A blurred motion to his left made him spin round, catching at the corner of his eye a second white blur as another one of the things dashed out of view. He raised a hand to his mouth, grimacing and fighting to keep down his supper upon seeing the mutilated bodies of Stanley's wife and one of the young men, their ravaged, bloody corpses showing signs of bite marks.

Insanity threatened to tear Richardson's mind apart. The harrowing horror, the bloody carnage and the madness battered and yammered at his brain, sending it spiralling in a hundred different directions, each one darker and more chaotic than the last.

"Are they gone?" asked one of the young men, shambling back into the light. His face was ashen and he was trembling. Blood ran from a claw mark on his arm.

"What in Hell's name were they?" questioned another. Unlike his friend he appeared uninjured but there was shock and confusion imprinted all over his face.

"I don't know—but we have to get out of here," answered Richardson. "It could be that the torchlight kept them away. We've got to get moving."

"I'm going nowhere without my husband. You've got to help him," pleaded Mary. She stood gazing down at her very dead husband, clearly not accepting the fact that he was beyond help, after all there was nothing in Richardson's first-aid kit that could perform miracles. "We have to get the police and an ambulance."

"Come on, let's get going before those things come back." One of the young men was practically pleading with Richardson to leave—to abandon the American woman if need be—after all he was the only one with a light source and this was now a survival situation. Tears would have to wait until they were out.

As Richardson hesitated, contemplating whether or not to drag the woman with him, there came the echoing clang of one of the portcullis-like gates closing. Several seconds later the sound came again, more muffled this time, further away and from a different direction.

"What was that?" asked Stanley. He had sat, huddled in a corner, his arms wrapped around his knees, his eyes wide and staring throughout the madness. Only now did he haul himself to his feet.

"I think they're trying to trap us; to block off our escape routes." Richardson swung his torch around, shining it over the three shadowy exits from the chamber they were in. It had sounded as though the way they had come was sealed off as well as one of the forward tunnels. "Those who want to see daylight again had better follow me." He waited, giving Mary the chance to join him if she so desired and was pleased to see her nod her head and shuffle forward, tears running down her face, smearing her make-up.

There were now only five of them, one of the young men still unaccounted for having fled into the darkness, presumably dead. They had set out as a group of ten—now they were half that number. All of them looked shell-shocked, weary, frightened and some were blood-spattered. There were glazed, disbelieving looks in their eyes, indicative of those who could not come to terms with what they had just experienced.

"Everyone stay close, keep moving and keep your eyes open." There was a determination in Richardson's stride as he set off down one of the passages—one which he hoped had not been blocked. His mind was a seething cauldron of writhing, chaotic thoughts but despite this he tried to mentally regain control, knowing that panic would not do him or any of the others any good. To succumb to the insanity would only compound the situation and would no doubt lead to them all getting killed. He forced himself to get a grip on his faculties; to think clearly and logically. He reckoned it would take them about ten minutes to reach an exit, providing it had not been blocked and that he could remain focused and remember the route.

They had been going for close on five minutes, the gnawing fear at what existed in the darkness and was no doubt in stealthy pursuit bordering on the unbearable.

Yet a little hope began to blossom in Richardson's chest as he firmly believed that he was heading in the right direction. The way had not been barred and the exit lay just ahead. When he got out he would head straight to the nearest police station and inform them of all that had happened. There were witnesses who would testify that he was telling the truth—no matter how incredible it might sound—that there were flesh-eating monsters, devils born of nightmare, haunting the Undercity.

"Keep moving. We're nearly out. Only another hundred yards or so."

It was then, when safety and salvation seemed to be tantalisingly within their grasp, that disaster struck as Richardson's torch went out again.

Scurrying forth from the impenetrable midnight blackness, the savage, child-sized mutant degenerates that had laired down in the deepest parts of the Undercity and the old sewage tunnels fell, ravenously, upon them. With teeth and claws they bore down on their screaming, vulnerable prey, tearing bloody gobbets of flesh from their still-living victims.

Richardson stumbled in the dark, one hand outstretched, reaching for a wall, supporting himself and managing to stay upright. There was nothing he could do for the others now. Only his own survival mattered. Swinging his silver-headed cane in fierce swipes, he edged away, each backward step bring him closer to the exit—or so he hoped.

The gurgling, chomping, slavering sounds that echoed all around were terrible. In his mind he envisaged those poor, hapless victims being torn apart and greedily devoured. He was thankful that he could not witness such gory proceedings.

Step-by-step, he kept retreating.

The sound of scrabbling and the patter of bare feet filled his ears and he was sure the horrors were approaching, no doubt readying themselves for an attack.

"Get back! Get back I warn you!"

"Sssh…sssh…feeeeed usss," cried out an unholy chorus of sibilant, unearthly voices. "Weeee…huuunger. Sssh…more… brrriing more."

Richardson's mind darkened.

"*More…*" came a pitiful wail; an ululation of the dammed.

A terrifying phantasmagoria of hideously laughing, wide-mouthed faces swam at him from out of the darkness, faces he recognised and had seen many times before. The painted faces of Charles Butterworth. And then a hellish realisation hit him and he knew why these ghouls of the Undercity had not attacked him; *had dared not attack him.* For his soul belonged to Butterworth, had done so for over two years when he had first set foot in that accursed room in 333 East Street. It had been that Satanist who had formed a pact with these creatures over a century before. He had been their feeder, providing them with morsels from above, until his execution. They still hungered and Butterworth's spectre had found a way to honour his pact, using Richardson to deliver unknowing victims to them, after all they preferred their meat fresh and as the majority of those he brought were visitors to the city, taking the tour on a whim, their disappearances had never led the police to Richardson. As a further measure, and to ensure no suspicion on the part of Richardson, Butterworth only took full possession after the creatures had claimed their victims, only entering the forefront of his host's soul and mind when the devilish deed was done.

With Butterworth now in full possession, Richardson found he could see in the dark. He could see that the ghouls were after more but they would have to wait for another night or two and even then it was rare that it was deemed safe enough for them to take an entire group as they had done on this occasion. They must have been starving, poor things. Whistling jauntily, he straightened his hat and made for the exit. In many ways, he was the greatest ghoul of the Undercity.

MASK OF THE OLMEC

A thing of ancient terror now stalked Oxford by night…

A large crowd had gathered outside the entrance to Christ Church college and Detective Inspector Mick Pearson was pleased to see that some of his men were already on the scene, keeping the onlookers back. A cordon had been set up and, as he got out of his car and made his way over, the bell of Tom Tower began tolling eight o'clock, its deep bonging sounding almost funereal in the overcast morning sunlight.

Pushing his way through the crowd, most of whom were students, he made his way into the quadrangle and over to the far corner.

Two police medics were busy putting their photographic equipment away under the supervision of an elderly man called Beswick, an extremely experienced forensic pathologist. One of his constables stood to one side, looking down at the white, blood-spattered sheet on the ground.

Swallowing a lump in his throat, Pearson strode over, hands in pockets. This was always the worst part of his job—viewing the recently deceased. Although not squeamish by nature, he would have been lying if he had said that he was all right with examining corpses, whether victims of natural death or other. Only yesterday he had been involved with fishing what was in all likelihood a suicide out of the Thames and that had definitely put him off his evening meal.

"It's not pretty," commented Beswick, crouching down and pulling the sheet away.

Pearson reeled back, his hand reaching for his mouth as he fought back the urge to vomit. The body had been torn apart as though by a wild animal. It was horribly mangled and he could see that the bloody corpse was incomplete. The head was missing.

"There are no visible footprints. Nor is there any circumstantial evidence apart from the body. Initial examination would suggest that the killer acted in a frenzied manner and although we've been unable to establish the nature of the murder weapon, I think it's obvious that excessive force was used." Beswick pointed to the grisly remains. "There are some strange lacerations and deep punctures to the thorax, left arm and buttocks which would seem to indicate animal claws, although—"

"*An animal!?* What do you mean? An escaped lion or something?"

"Maybe, but there have been no reported sightings."

"Nevertheless, check into it. I know there's a circus based up at University Parks. Perhaps—"

"Sir!"

Pearson turned to where his constable stood several feet away. "What is it?"

"Look!" The constable pointed to the ivy-covered wall of the college building. "Is that just my imagination or are there bloodstains there. *See?* They start about ten feet up and then continue right up the wall towards the roof."

Pearson squinted and looked to where the other indicated. There were indeed blood stains visible; dark-red splotches on the old, coarse brickwork. There were windows nearby but it appeared that the trail bypassed them, leading up to the roof. Walking over to the wall, he saw that brick fragments and loose chippings lay in a small pile at the base; all indicative of something having scaled the wall, no doubt carrying the missing bits of its savaged victim.

"It would appear that our killer's quite the athlete," commented Beswick, gauging the climb. "As there doesn't appear to be any prints close to the body I think it's a possibility that the attack may have come from on high."

"Are you saying that whatever did this jumped from up there on to the victim? Removed the head—"

"Liver, lungs, stomach and kidneys."

Pearson grimaced. "And then what? Climbed back up?"

"I'd say it's a possibility."

"Do we have an I.D. of the victim?"

"Obviously male. Early twenties. Nothing definite as yet, however the college is doing a roll-call, so if he were a student here we should find out soon."

"If this were a murder as opposed to an animal attack do you have any suggestions as to motive?"

Beswick shook his head. "Hard to say. If we rule out an animal attack, I'd guess either we've got a psychopathic trophy collector on our hands or a god-dammed cannibal."

"What about time of death?"

"From the fact that the blood has congealed somewhat and the stage of rigor mortis, I would say sometime after midnight."

"Any witnesses?"

"None so far, but I'm pretty sure that once we've established identity, we'll be able to form a much clearer picture."

Beswick hesitated upon seeing an approaching constable.

"Yes, what is it?" asked Pearson.

"Sir, there's a report of another victim. The details suggest a definite similarity."

"Where?"

"Down by the Botanical Gardens. The body was discovered only ten minutes ago." The constable gulped. "It would appear to be headless as well. There has also been a sighting. It's a bit unclear, sir, but the witness reported seeing a dark, man-shaped shadow with glowing green eyes and...fangs. Whatever this thing was it was spotted on the top of a lamp-post on the High Street, apparently munching at something."

* * * *

It was now eleven o'clock and Pearson sat at his desk filling in paperwork pertaining to the two brutal killings. He was deeply troubled, having never encountered anything like this before. The barbarity of the slayings had shocked him despite his twenty-five years in his chosen career and having investigated numerous murder cases. Stabbings, shootings, drownings—they had all been relatively easy to cope with compared to this, which sickened him to the core. His revulsion had been intensified when Beswick had suggested that the blood-rich organs that had been removed had possibly been devoured—a theory which had been strengthened when they had examined the second body and heard the witness statement. Once more they had found a trail of blood and strewn viscera leading away from the severely mutilated corpse.

Pearson felt queasy and tried to erase those horrible images from his mind. He had to remain focused. There was a ruthless, no doubt insane, killer at large and it was his problem to solve.

Positive identification of the two unfortunates had been made. The remains found on the college grounds were those of Oliver Westwood. Those at the Botanical Gardens, Peter Davis. What was more, there was a connection for both had been students at the University, both reading archaeology and anthropology. Pearson had already left a message with the senior tutor, one Professor Otto Möller, an expert in Mesoamerican archaeology.

Next of kin had been informed and Pearson's next step was to face the reporters who were already clamouring for details. Rumours were spreading throughout the student population and would soon leak out into the wider community and when that happened there could well be widespread panic. Although exact details of the deaths had been strictly downplayed it wouldn't be possible to keep the grisly nature of the killings away from the inquisitive.

Taking a sip of coffee, Pearson was about to return to his form filling when his phone started ringing. He picked it up.

"Could I speak to Detective Inspector Pearson?" There was an unmistakable German undertone to the caller's voice.

"Speaking. How can I help?"

"Ah, Inspector, this is Professor Otto Möller. I understand that you wanted to speak to me in relation to the most tragic events of today."

"That's correct, Professor Möller. Obviously you understand that all of this is just purely routine but I was wondering if I could come around and see you sometime this afternoon? I would also appreciate it if you could, in the meantime, make a list of the names of any of the two victims' friends and associates so that I can arrange for interviews."

"I'll certainly do all that I can to assist. Would two o'clock be a convenient time?"

"Fine. I'll see you then." Pearson put down the phone. Wiggling his pen between his teeth, he stared at his paperwork, wondering just what to write in the 'cause of death' slot. The pathologist, Beswick, was still uncertain, toying with the theory that it may have been a wild animal, a terribly savage and undoubtedly feral dog for example. As explanations went it was reasonable up to a point, but it didn't explain the wall climbing or the nature of the head removal from the victims.

There were so many things that had him completely at a loss and it was only with a great level of mental restraint that he kept his theorising away from the realms of the supernatural. After all, to an ignorant and superstitious mind, the attacks displayed certain hallmarks of werewolf activity. With that thought uncomfortably lodged in his mind, he glanced across at his wall calendar and his heart skipped a beat when he saw that last night had been the time of the full moon.

* * * *

"Inspector, do come in. I only wish our meeting was under better circumstances." Möller held the door to his cluttered office open and admitted the other, gesturing to a padded chair by the fireplace.

"Professor." Pearson gave a curt nod and entered, taking his seat.

Möller was a tall, thin, white-haired man with a monocle covering his left eye. He had to be close on retirement age. A typical product of Oxford, he seemed every bit the erudite eccentric, dressed in his tweeds and bowtie. He reached into a drawer in his desk and took out a brandy decanter and two large glasses.

"Not for me, thanks," said Pearson.

Möller looked disappointed. With a shrug of his shoulders, he returned one glass and filled his own.

"Well. I'm sure you appreciate and understand the severity of this terrible occurrence." Pearson gazed around him at the confines of the small office. There were several bookcases, cabinets filled with strange artefacts and more than a few large wall maps.

"Of course, most terrible. I've already sent out my condolences to the parents via the academic secretary attached to the college and as I said on the phone, I'm more than happy to offer whatever assistance is requested."

Möller took a drink from his glass before taking a piece of paper from his in-tray and passing it over. "Here's the list of all those in the same year, as well as the names of friends and the like, as far as I could discover."

"I appreciate it." Pearson gave the list a cursory glance before putting it in his pocket. "I understand that you're an expert on Mesoamerican archaeology. Forgive my ignorance, but I take it that's all about the Incas and the like, yes?"

"No, I'm afraid not. The Incas were a South American civilisation, a sovereign political entity that developed from the Andean cultures located mainly in Peru. My field of speciality concerns the incipient Mesoamerican civilisations, primarily that of the Olmec culture which flourished in the Gulf lowlands of Mexico around two and a half to three thousand years ago. An extremely fascinating people who were to lay down the foundations for many subsequent Mesoamerican civilisations, notably the Toltec, Mayan and of course the Aztec, which I take it you've heard of?"

"I've heard of them but I know next to nothing about them. I'm afraid there's not much call for knowledge like that in the police. Still, sounds like fascinating stuff." Pearson reached into a jacket pocket, removed a small notebook and a pen. "Can you tell me anything about the two young men? How were they academically, for example?"

"Both were exceptionally gifted students. Oliver in particular. I'm certain that they would have had very bright and promising futures had this terrible thing not happened. In fact, they had only recently returned from a field-trip to Mexico led by Doctor Wilson where I believe they made some significant discoveries."

"Doctor Wilson?" Pearson jotted the name down.

"Yes, Doctor Stephanie Wilson. She teaches over at the Institute although she spends most of her time at the Ashmolean Museum where she's the curator for the Mesoamerican Archaeological department. I've informed her of what's happened and as you can no doubt imagine she was very shocked to hear the news." Möller frowned and puckered his lips. It was clear that he wanted to ask a question but was uncertain how exactly to frame it. In the end, he decided to just come straight out with it. "Inspector, the accounts that I've been hearing suggest that these deaths were…rather grisly in nature and that, well, some are saying that they go way beyond anything that could be classed as a normal killing, if indeed there is such a thing."

"I'm afraid so. For not only were both bodies torn apart but as yet we've been unable to find their heads." Noticing the strange way in which his answer seemed to affect the professor, Pearson leant across the desk. "Does this mean anything to you?"

Möller had become noticeably jittery. With the back of his hand he wiped a sheen of sweat from his brow. "Maybe, maybe not."

"If you know anything I'd like to hear it." Pearson's voice hardened and his eyes narrowed.

Möller let out a long sigh. "There's a legend—"

"I'm not interested in legends, professor. Only facts, hard evidence that I can see and examine."

"Please, just hear me out. It might have a bearing, it might not. But, as I was saying, there's a legend prevalent among many of the incipient Mesoamerican cultures concerning the werejaguar; a potent, religious anthropomorphic beast that—"

"I haven't come here to listen to nonsense." Pearson interrupted with a dismissive wave of his hand. "So why don't you keep your myths and monsters to the lecture hall? Two young men have been brutally slain not five hundred yards from this room and I don't have the time to hear you talk about things that don't exist."

"I'm just trying to help. Besides, it was you who asked me to tell you anything I knew that might have relevance."

"All right, let's hear it." Pearson sighed.

"There's one legend of the werejaguar that I think, considering the bizarre circumstances, to be of particular interest." Möller paused, uncertain exactly how to continue now that the detective was prepared to listen. The theory that had begun to form in his own mind went way beyond his wildest dreams. All the time he had been investigating the ancient civilisations and the cults of the long-dead, he had wondered whether or not there had ever been any truth in the old legends. For they all spoke of a hidden world beyond that which ordinary mortals could see or interact with; a world inhabited by devils and demons that plagued the lives of men whenever they stepped across the dividing line, or were conjured by spells and incantations. "This legend, which has been passed down through countless generations and is certainly prevalent in Olmec myth, specifically concerns the taking of heads from the slain. Why this was done remains a mystery, but one need only look to such things as the *tzompantli*—the skull racks predominant throughout various Mesoamerican cultures—to appreciate its ritual significance. Some of the less well-known legends tell of how the shamans would manufacture figurines of werejaguars and breathe life into them, making them assume actual form. They would then be dispatched to kill their enemies."

"I take it that this werejaguar's a bit like a werewolf?" Pearson tensed, remembering his discovery that last night had been the night of the full moon, the night when such creatures—lycanthropes—were said to be most active.

"Well yes, but whereas the werewolf is primarily a Northern European folkloric monster usually spawned from the beliefs of the superstitious peasant stock; the werejaguar, certainly amongst the ancients of Mesoamerica, was raised to an almost god-like status. It was worshipped, not necessarily vilified. It's my belief that the werejaguars as depicted on numerous statues...talking of which, I believe I have one in my cabinet. Excuse me one moment." Möller got to his feet and went to a glass-fronted display cabinet on the wall. Removing a key from his jacket pocket, he opened it and took out a small green figurine. He handed it over.

Pearson studied the statuette. "Doesn't look much like a jaguar."

"Indeed. Personally, it's my opinion that it's a depiction of a shamanistic figure. Note the down-turned mouth and the almond-shaped eyes. I think rather than an actual human-animal composite what we have here is more of a symbolic attempt to convey jaguar-like abilities onto a human form. I hold to the view that the ancient Olmec religious leaders, the shamans, were being portrayed as possessing animal characteristics, not dissimilar to the early Egyptian god-kings."

"I'm afraid I'm none the wiser." Pearson passed the figurine back. "I mean, are you telling me that it's your belief that it's one of these hideous creatures that is now running amok in Oxford, collecting the heads of its victims for some kind of weird ritualistic purpose?"

"That's not what I'm saying, Inspector. I mean, it doesn't take a genius to see the incredulity in your eyes. No doubt you'd think me a raving lunatic if I began to espouse such theories. No, I'm merely telling you that, as far-fetched as it sounds, I think it's a possibility. Or it could be some sick individual trying to copy the legends. All I'm doing is providing you with the details and the link, that's all. Obviously, it's up to you what to do with the information I've provided. May I suggest a visit to Doctor Wilson if you wish to pursue this line of enquiry further as she is more clued up on such things than I am."

* * * *

On his short walk back to the police headquarters, Pearson was dismayed to see that the newspaper sellers were already out, informing all and sundry that there was a '*monster*' at large. There was a sense of fear and apprehension in the air, something he had, in all his years of policing, never detected before. It was almost like a tangible wave, something that seemed to have descended over the university city like a death shroud.

Turning off the main street, where the growing autumnal wind blew cold and chill, flapping his coat around him, he stepped into a cobbled alley that led to Christ Church Meadow. Despite the overall pleasantness of his surroundings, he shivered as strange thoughts went through his head. He had always prided himself on the ability to look at things objectively, to dismiss in his mind the existence of the weird and the wonderful. And yet, more so after his conversation with the professor, he found himself now dealing with something he had never considered before. He had never believed in such fantasies as ghosts and demons. They had absolutely no place in his life. He dealt only with those things that he could see and feel. Now, his mind was floundering, out of its depth, groping for something firm and sane on which it could anchor itself, to reinstate sanity in a situation that had the potential of becoming increasingly insane.

Olmecs! Werejaguars! Stolen heads! He would have laughed at the idea that there was any kind of connection had he been able to establish an alternative explanation behind the terrible double murders. But the harsh fact remained that there was still an extremely violent killer at large—human or otherwise—and as things currently stood he was no closer to tracking them down. He had wondered whether or not it would be for the best to put out a general alert to the public, perhaps enforce a student curfew until the killer had been apprehended. It was not something that could be done easily nor was it an act that he would do willingly for that was, in some way, tantamount to an admittance that the police could no longer fulfil their duty in keeping the public safe and his heart sank when he considered the possible repercussions. It was a difficult one, for if by his inaction there was another victim…

A light drizzle began to fall from the darkening skies and it was with a shudder that Pearson realised that there was not another single soul in sight. Normally the park was filled with people; students and tourists mainly, but this afternoon it was empty apart from himself. The unsettling notion that there was something unnatural out there somewhere, perhaps nearby, skulking in the bushes or perched in the treetops, made him quicken his stride. A dull, sick sensation filled his stomach and he looked quickly behind him to ensure that nothing unwholesome was creeping up on him, ready to clamp its clawed fingers around his throat and rip his head from his shoulders.

There was nothing there.

With a shake of his head, Pearson shrugged away his dark thoughts and drew his coat tighter. He came to the path that led out to the park and, thankfully, the feeling of fear lessened in his mind. It was as if the dark thoughts that had been plaguing him and the memory of the gruesome corpses he had seen earlier that morning had suddenly left and there was only the gusting wind.

* * * *

It had just gone half-past four by the time Pearson completed his initial report on the two deaths and the police station had become a hub of activity. Several more detectives had been assigned to the case and a dozen or so officers had been drafted in from several of the neighbouring towns.

Pearson had managed to delegate a colleague to stand in his place for a specially convened press report. From where he sat, in his office, he could hear the clamouring of people in the lobby, no doubt investigative reporters seeking more information. Apart from the one alleged sighting of something 'shadowy and man-like with glaring eyes and large, fanged teeth' perched atop a lamp-post there was nothing really to go on.

A sudden worried thought struck him and he cursed himself for not having thought of it earlier. Were there any other student members of the field-trip to Mexico? And if so, were they now in danger? He reached for his phone book and found the number for Doctor Wilson at the Ashmolean Museum.

After six rings the phone was picked up.

"Doctor Wilson."

"Hello, this is Detective Inspector Mick Pearson. I hope I'm not calling at an inconvenient time, but I think you know why I'm phoning."

"Yes, yes. Indeed I do. A most appalling tragedy. Truly horrible. Have you by chance caught whoever was responsible? Pray tell me you have."

"I'm afraid not. I'm calling to enquire about the field-trip to Mexico that both men had recently returned from. An expedition that I understand you led. Could you tell me a bit more about it?"

"Why certainly, Inspector. I'd be more than happy to. Do you want me to come to the police station in order to make a statement or would it be all right over the phone?"

"Why don't I come round to the museum? Things are becoming a little hectic here. Shall we say, half an hour?"

"Very good."

"I'll see you soon." Pearson put the phone down. There was a knock on his door. "Come in."

Beswick, the forensic pathologist, entered, a medical clipboard in his hand. "You're not going to believe this. Hell, I don't know whether I believe it or not."

"What have you got?"

Beswick sat down. "I've done all of the routine tests on the two bodies. As you know they're largely incomplete, missing most of the main internal organs as well as their heads. However, I've also found several strange hair fibres, which are clearly non-human. Tests indicate that the closest correlation is to the *Panthera* genus—"

"A big cat?" Pearson felt the lump in his throat as he asked the question.

"Yes, exactly. Now we've been in touch with all of the nearby zoos, circuses and even one or two private owners of wild cats but they're all accounted for."

"Do you think it could have been a jaguar?"

"Could be, although the method of predation would suggest something bigger."

"How conclusive are your test results?"

"Well, that's just it. They're not. At least not one hundred percent and that's where most of the problem lies. Normally, I'd be able to tell you exactly what kind of creature we're dealing with. But not in this case. Now, I wouldn't go so far as to suggest that this thing is a hitherto unknown species or something outrageous like a werewolf, however—"

"Wouldn't you?" Pearson interrupted, a deeply troubled look on his face.

Beswick read the thoughtfulness in the other's eyes, the level of seriousness with which he had asked his question. It came as something of a relief, for he too harboured such notions but he had been reluctant to make them known for fear of ridicule. "I'll be honest with you, Mick, I don't know what we've got out there."

"Do you believe in such things? I mean, is there any place for such horrors in your scientific view of the world?"

"Of course there's room but as you know, as a scientist, I need evidence." Beswick coughed. "Unfortunately that cuts both ways and I can't ignore the evidence lying downstairs in the police morgue. Two headless cadavers, torn apart by an unknown agency. It's unlike anything I've ever seen before and I have been in this business a long time now."

"Let's just assume, for a moment, that we are dealing with something like a werewolf. I mean, what are we looking at? Silver bullets and all that kind of stuff?"

"Your guess is as good as mine. I too noticed that last night was the night of the full moon. And that's when these things are supposed to come out, isn't it? I guess we'll have to hope that if it is a werewolf then perhaps its hunting cycle is precluded to but one night a month. If that's the case we've got a month or so until this monster becomes active once more. The last thing we need is for this creature to be out on the prowl every night. To be honest, I don't think we should inform anyone else of our suspicions. I'm looking forward to my pension not the inside of a loony bin."

"Yes. I agree." Pearson rose from his chair. "Anyway, I've got an appointment with someone at the Ashmolean. A Doctor Wilson. She was the team leader for the expedition that the two students went on to Mexico. I guess there's a part of me that just hopes there's not a connection."

"I wouldn't have thought they'd get werewolves out in Mexico. Now if you'd said that they'd just returned from Transylvania or somewhere like that…"

"Not werewolves. Werejaguars." The Detective Inspector put on his coat. "I'll see you later. Tomorrow probably. Give me a call if you find out any more."

* * * *

Pearson saw Doctor Wilson waiting at the entrance to the museum and although the two had never met before he picked her out quite easily as she was the only academic-looking person there.

"Detective Inspector Pearson."

"You must be Doctor Wilson, yes?"

"That's correct. Please, follow me." Doctor Wilson was fifty-seven, small and grey-haired with a deeply tanned face. She wore glasses and walked with a noticeable limp in her right leg. However, there was an alert, almost vibrant look to her, suggestive of someone who had done a lot of travelling to strange and exotic places.

"It was Professor Möller who suggested that I come to see you," said Pearson as they walked down one of the long, statue-lined galleries. "He told me about your expedition to Mexico."

"Indeed. Well, why don't I tell you about it in my office. We're nearly there now." Doctor Wilson removed a key from her pocket and unlocked a door. Entering a stretch of short corridor, she led the detective down a flight of stairs and into a large room where numerous unopened crates and boxes and pieces of statuary resided. There were several glass cabinets half-filled with various ancient Mesoamerican relics.

"I take it this material is not yet on public display?" Pearson asked.

"No. Not yet. I've got a lot of cataloguing and classifying to do before we get to that stage. Most of these items are on loan from the museum at Tres Zapotes, close to where we were working, carrying out some important investigative archaeological work. Unfortunately, what with the terrible loss of two of the Institute's most gifted students, I'm sure we're not going to reach our deadline for unveiling this display." Doctor Wilson opened a door. "Here we are. Please, do take a seat."

The office Pearson entered was small and musty, filled with all manner of bizarre items in cabinets. There were books, scrolls, maps, posters, pieces of pottery and photographs everywhere. One such photograph on the desk showed a somewhat younger-looking Doctor Wilson posing beside a colossal, squat stone head with thick puffy lips and a somewhat flattened, boxer's nose.

Doctor Wilson sat down and reached into a drawer. "I have here the list of those students who accompanied me to Mexico." She handed it over.

"Thanks." Pearson read the names of the deceased and ran a finger down the names of the three others scribbled below.

"Do you think they may be in danger?"

Pearson looked at the list a moment longer. "I'm afraid I can't say. The connection is tenuous at best but as things currently stand it's all I've got to go by. When I get back to the station I'll see about putting out a warning, just to be on the safe side. Now, I don't want to worry you unduly, but—"

"But I too could be in danger, yes?" Doctor Wilson fixed the detective with a hard stare. "For the life of me I can't understand who would want to do such a thing. It makes no sense whatsoever."

"Doctor Wilson." Pearson decided it was high time to come right out with it. "Forgive me for questioning your expertise but I take it that you're familiar with the legend of the werejaguar?"

"The werejaguar? Why, of course. It was a fairly common motif used by the Olmecs and several of the later Mesoamerican cultures. There are numerous depictions and statuettes of were-jaguars in various guises. Why, in this collection alone there are plenty of jade and serpentine werejaguar figurines, including werejaguar babies and one or two which display the actual transformation process between man and beast."

"Now this might sound strange and believe me I'd be the first to admit it, but do you think that such a creature exists?"

"What?" Dr Wilson looked at Pearson as though he was mad. "Are you trying to tell me that you think a werejaguar murdered those young men? Please, Inspector, I don't take you for a fool so don't take me for one either. There are no such things as werejaguars outside of the ancient artwork of a people long gone; vanished, dead now for over two thousand years."

"I wish that were true but the evidence would seem to suggest otherwise. I've got two young men, murdered, torn to pieces, their heads removed and I don't know what the hell's responsible."

"You, you said that their heads were removed?"

"Yes. Professor Möller told me about the ritual significance behind this. He wouldn't rule out the possibility that whatever did this was not natural in origin."

"I'm afraid I don't share those beliefs. Nobody sane would."

"Maybe you're right." A sudden sense of futility struck Pearson. Odds were he was barking up the wrong tree, indeed the more he thought about it, he had to be, for the alternative surely bordered on the ludicrous. With a sigh, he got to his feet. "Very well, Doctor Wilson, if anything should occur to you that you think I should know I'd appreciate it if you got in touch. Thank you for your time. I'll make my own way out."

* * * *

It was nearing eight o'clock. Pearson sat in his office, having just finished a heated phone conversation with his wife, telling her that there was something mighty weird going on and as a consequence he would be working late. He felt tired, after all it had been a long day and he had drank six cups of coffee since returning from his meeting with Doctor Wilson in an attempt to stay focused and alert.

Extra police officers, some of them armed, had been put on the streets and he had managed to get in touch with all but one of the remaining students on the list, informing them, for their own safety, to be extra vigilant and to stay indoors where possible. The student he had been unable to contact, one Carlos Ramirez, a native Mexican who had come to Oxford to study, was apparently visiting family in London and wouldn't be back for several days.

There was a knock on his office door.

"Come in."

The door was opened by one of his constables. Alongside him, looking haggard, pale-faced and frightened was Professor Möller.

"Professor, do come in." Pearson looked to his constable. "Get him a coffee, would you?"

"Yes, sir." The dispatched policeman walked away.

Möller nervously entered. He was visibly shaking and he held a tattered brown briefcase in his knobbly hands. Gone now was the self-assured, if slightly odd-looking academic Pearson had encountered earlier that day. For he now appeared like a man who had barely escaped from Hell and at some terrible cost. His eyes were wide and staring.

"Are you all right?"

"It's, it's *her*. Wilson. *She's* the werejaguar." Möller's voice was wavering. "I stopped by the museum just as it was closing. I had some papers to collect from her office. I—" He stared about him with wide eyes as though half-expecting something mad and snarling to come crashing through the upper story window or else burst out of the filing cabinet.

"What is it? Come on, snap out of it man!"

"*Wilson's* the beast. She killed those two students."

"Are you sure? I mean, what makes you think that?"

"*Their heads!* Their heads were in her closet. I found their heads in her closet." Möller was bordering on the hysterical.

"Good God!"

With hands that were visibly trembling, the professor opened his briefcase. "There's more. I found her notebook." Reaching inside, he then handed over a black, bound book. "It tells about her excavations on the outskirts of Tres Zapotes and how she unearthed one of the Olmec mounds. Inside, she found a devilish jade mask, one that would transform the wearer into an animal, a werejaguar."

Pearson was only half-listening, preoccupied with skimming through the written details, having trouble reading the spidery handwriting.

"In her last few entries she makes it clear that she planned to do more research into the masks and how she would have to slay those who had been present at the excavation of the mound and the discovery of the mask. That is, the remaining students. She plans to kill them all."

"Do you know where she is now?"

"She'll either be at the museum, and if so she'll no doubt have discovered that someone's stolen her notebook, or she'll be at her house in North Oxford. I've got her address—"

The office door was flung wide. "Sir, we've got a sighting of something down by the Bodleian Library."

Despite his fatigue, Pearson was up in a shot. "Gather some men and make sure they're armed." He looked to Möller. "If you know anything that might be useful in battling this monster I'd like you to come with me. Otherwise, I think it best that you remain here."

"I see no reason why a gun wouldn't kill it. But, I'll gladly come with you."

"Right. Let's go!"

* * * *

Pearson heard the shots being fired before he arrived on the scene. Parking on the High Street, he and Möller got out and made their way towards the Radcliffe Camera. Clinging to the moon-thrown shadows, they crept to the end of the side-street and peered out in shocked amazement as half a dozen policemen marksmen, armed with high-powered rifles aimed and shot at something crouched low near the top of the monument.

"What's happening?" asked Pearson, running over to join one of the policemen.

"We've got whatever it is pinned down on the roof. It's a weird thing, no doubt about that. It's jumping around like nothing I've ever seen before." The man took aim and squeezed the trigger. He either missed or his shot had little impact. "If I didn't know better I'd say it's either Spring-Heeled Jack or a bloody werewolf."

Pearson tried hard to make out the thing that had now blended into the shadows, making itself nigh on invisible. He was certain that it was still up there for the structure was isolated from any others and surely even a creature like this was incapable of leaping over a hundred yards to reach the next nearest building.

"It may be able to make its way inside through a skylight," reasoned Möller.

"Well as far as I'm aware there is no one inside nor are there any alternative escape routes. So even if it were to get inside we still have it contained."

Suddenly a black shadow seemed to detach itself from a low wall high up on the roof. More shots rang out as it scaled down a part of the edifice before springing the remaining distance, a jump of over thirty feet. It landed nimbly and took off at a tremendous pace, swiping its way past one policeman who tried in vain to shoot it. The man fell to the ground, his face clawed open.

"Don't let it get away!" Pearson shouted, joining the mad rush as he and his men gave pursuit.

Into the darkened cobbled backstreets went the policemen, their weapons no longer that effective, their rifles much more suited for far-range targeting.

There came a scream from up ahead, and a few seconds later two young women came running out of the darkness. The armed policeman moved forward, telling them to get out, that there was a wild animal at large.

"Inspector, wait up!"

Pearson turned upon hearing the professor's call.

There came a shot from over to his right and then a cry. For one terrible moment he was certain he saw a dark shape slip across an alley opening. There were more screams followed by a horrible ripping sound. A policeman staggered forth before falling to the ground, his left arm now a bloody stump.

Gunfire, screams and the sound of approaching police sirens filled the night. There was chaos now as the vicious monster, unable to target its intended victims, directed its wrath to all and sundry. It was a remorseless killer, an age-old fiend that delighted in slaying and feasting. Without real regard for its own safety, it lunged across the busy High Street, vaulting over passing cars and knocking cyclists off their bikes. Two drunks who had just left one of the nearby pubs tried to stop it. Both died horribly for their act of alcohol-induced stupidity.

It was blatantly clear to Pearson that he wasn't going to catch this thing, especially not with the aged Möller trying to keep up with him. "Damn!" he cursed savagely.

"My guess is it would make for the Museum. Wilson will no doubt go there and remove the mask, make herself normal again."

"Too obvious. If she knows that we've got her notebook I'd be more inclined to think that she's gone to her house, maybe to get ready to flee the country. Perhaps she intends to go back to Mexico with that accursed thing. If you know where she lives then direct me there. Quick, let's get back to the car."

* * * *

Pearson had picked up a fallen rifle belonging to one of his deceased officers and it now rested on the back seat as he sped towards Wilson's house. On either side of the road loomed large Victorian houses, with big gardens and most of the properties were walled off from their neighbours. It was an area of the city preserved largely for university lecturers and professors and as such it housed an eclectic mix of eccentric, intellectual types.

"Next left, I think. Wilson's house is the big one at the end of the next turning."

They pulled over and both got out.

Rifle in hand, Pearson stepped silently, trying to throw his vision into the dark, for the streetlight was poor, shedding little illumination on this side of the street and there were no house lights on. Everything was still and shadowy. He stopped to listen. All was silent.

"Do you really think she'd have come back here?" whispered Möller.

"Shh!" Pearson's heart was now thumping madly in his chest and there was a nervous apprehension festering in the pit of his stomach. An uncomfortable icy dampness crept down his spine and he felt the sweaty feel on his hands where he grasped the rifle. He couldn't remember the last time he had ever properly held a gun, never mind fired one.

Like shadows themselves they crept into the garden and headed for the back door. It was wide open.

The room beyond was clearly a kitchen and Pearson was just about to go inside when he spotted what looked like bloodstains on the patio steps. After pointing them out to Möller, he sneaked inside, ready and more than willing to open fire on anything that might emerge from the dark confines of the room.

The tick-tock of a wall clock sounded over to his left.

Möller flicked a switch and sudden light chased away the shadows.

The kitchen was nondescript and had it not been for the thick red blotches on the linoleum it would have been perfectly normal in appearance. The trail led from the back door to the open door straight in front of them.

Pearson's heart lurched and his eyes narrowed upon hearing a creak from directly overhead. He was in two minds about calling out, hoping that Doctor Wilson would appear, lambasting them for their intrusion but doing little more. There was a gut-wrenching tug in his stomach, a deep-rooted sense of fear that temporarily paralysed him. Marshalling his courage, he advanced into the hallway beyond. There was a thick carpet covering the floor and several small paintings adorned the walls. At the end of the hall, the stairs up ascended into darkness.

Noiselessly, they moved along the corridor, tense now, alert to the sounds in the house, which had suddenly become noticeable. Slowly, they made their way to the stairs, eyes turned upward, expectant and alert. But nothing appeared there.

Straining his senses, Pearson fancied he heard the almost imperceptible sound of something panting. As he stood there, with Möller taut and quivering beside him, he could feel the impression of malevolence about him like the hot breath of some carnivorous animal, poised to leap. For a long moment, he stood undecided, struggling to focus as fear clamped down on his mind. He absolutely dreaded the thought of going any further, of disturbing this house and its horrible secrets. He could sense that something was watching him, gauging his movements in readiness to pounce from the shadows. A trickle of cold seat ran down the side of his face. His hands were shaking and he now knew what it must be like to a be a big-game hunter out in the jungle somewhere, knowing that he might have but one good shot before the beast was upon him. *But would a normal bullet prove effective?* Desperately, he tried to push that unsettling question away.

Reaching out, he trailed his hand down the wall, locating the light switch. He flicked it.

Nothing happened! The stairs and the landing remained dark, threatening.

Suddenly there came a deep-throated growl and the were-jaguar sprang from where it had been hiding in the closet under the stairs. In a blur of movement, it grabbed Möller and dashed him to the floor, blood streaming from the horribly scratched marks gouged deep into his arms. It then withdrew into the kitchen, presenting the detective with a good target, silhouetted as it was against the light.

Never in his wildest nightmares had Pearson seen such a strange and dreadful monster. Standing upright on two legs and roughly man-sized in shape, the horror's fur was yellow with brown spots, its underbelly mostly white. Its arms were spread wide, terminating in vicious claws that looked as though they could tear through hardened cement. A long tail sprouted from its rear end. But it was its head that was by far the strangest. For whereas Pearson had half-expected it to have been that of a large, bloody-mawed, green-eyed jaguar, it was in actuality an ugly jade mask, its facial features similar to some of the Olmec figurines he had seen previously; puffy, snarling lips and almond-shaped eyes.

He raised his rifle and pulled the trigger.

The bullet took the lycanthrope full in the chest, knocking it further into the kitchen whereupon it crashed against the sink. Smashing a pile of plates and cups on to the floor, it started to haul itself back to its feet. It had clearly been wounded, viscous black-red blood streaming from where it had been hit.

Pearson advanced, levelled the rifle and took a second shot, blasting the werejaguar once more in the chest, sending it reeling. He was pleased to see that normal bullets were having such an effect. Without mercy, he fired a third time, killing the beast instantly.

Bleeding profusely, Möller crawled over. "Did you get it?" he managed to ask.

"Yes. I'm sure it's dead." Gun trained on it in case it should move, Pearson strode towards its body. It was a truly ghastly thing, unsightly, unnatural. But thankfully it was no longer breathing.

"There's bound to be a knife in one of those drawers. Remove the mask."

Pearson nodded and opened a drawer. Taking out a large kitchen knife, he went down on one knee and lifted the monster's head. A thick leather strap secured the mask to the head. It didn't take long to saw through it and, with an apprehensive gulp, he lifted the jade relic free. In stunned amazement, he found himself looking down not at the grey-haired and haggard face of Doctor Wilson—for her mutilated, headless corpse was lying upstairs—but rather at a tanned, dark-haired young man with piercing blue eyes.

"My God! It's Carlos Ramirez!" exclaimed Möller, disbelievingly. "He was the werejaguar. He must've falsified that notebook, hoping to incriminate Doctor Wilson. He planted those heads in her office so that, so that—" The loss of blood suddenly overtaking him, he collapsed.

Pearson couldn't remember where he had heard that name and, with his mind in a turmoil at recent events, he did not care. At this precise moment in time he had something more important to do. Repeatedly, he brought the mask down hard, on the kitchen table, cracking it, then smashing it to pieces.

THE CONTRACT

*For Daniel Hoogstratten, the Devil
really was in the detail...*

Private Investigator Vincent Carmichael stepped out of his office on a bright, sunny Friday afternoon and straight into what was to become a nightmare. Prior to the moment he became acquainted with Daniel Hoogstratten, his life had been free of anything even remotely bordering on the unnatural and the inexplicable; forty-four years of blissful ignorance, sheltered from the true horrors that he was about to confront. He had prided himself on his outlook, his staunch philosophy—one that denied the possibility of the weird and that, even in as strange and crazy a city as Los Angeles, had done wonders in preserving his sanity.

He turned when a hand grabbed his right shoulder.

"Mr. Carmichael?" The hand's owner was a tall, thin, grey-haired man, his face browned by exposure to the sun, worn and criss-crossed with numerous worry lines. There was a strangely haunted look in his deep-set eyes and he had the appearance of a man who rarely, if ever, smiled. He was dressed in a baggy black suit that was several sizes too big for him and in the hand that didn't grasp Carmichael's shoulder he held a black briefcase.

"Yes, that's me."

The hand was removed. The action done slowly, with a wince, as though the movement pained the dark-suited stranger. "It's very important that—"

"I'm sorry but I've got a train to catch. If you've got anything you want investigated why don't you get in touch with my secretary? Now, if you don't mind—" Carmichael made to push past the other.

"I have to see you now. It's very important."

"So's my train. Look, Mister…?"

"Hoogstratten. Daniel Hoogstratten."

"Mr. Hoogstratten. If you've got any business then—"

Hoogstratten rested his briefcase on the pavement, reached into an inner suit pocket and removed a chequebook and a black fountain pen. "How much? A hundred dollars? Two hundred? I implore you. You're my last hope."

"Can't this wait till Monday?" Carmichael was becoming tetchy now. Part of him was eager to be off so that he could catch his train out into the suburbs where he lived and he knew that if he missed this he would have to wait another two hours for the next one. The other part of him was intrigued as to just what this old man wanted from him. Money was nice but it wasn't really the main incentive for him. He took satisfaction in unravelling the case, discovering the undiscovered and solving that which many thought unsolvable.

"It just can't. I'll explain everything. Please—"

Carmichael gave a deep, resigned sigh. "Very well. Follow me." Re-entering the building, he led the other through the main reception room, passing his secretary with a tired nod of his head. The two men then entered the elevator and were soon ascending up several floors.

Not a word was spoken.

During that uncomfortable silence, Carmichael detected an embarrassing and distinctly unpleasant odour coming from the other. It was a sharp, vinegar-like smell mingled with something nutty as of rotting fruit spread atop a coating of peanut butter. And that was not all, for Hoogstratten kept twitching involuntarily, his juddering becoming more erratic as he jittered from one foot to the other. His lips trembled but he said nothing.

The elevator door opened and they stepped out.

"My office is the first on the right." Carmichael walked over to a coffee dispensing machine. "You want a drink?" he asked.

Hoogstratten declined with a shake of his head.

"Suit yourself." Once Carmichael had got his coffee, he took a drink, painfully swallowing the piping hot liquid. Opening the door to his office, he stepped inside. He was about to take his seat behind his desk, aware that Hoogstratten had followed him in, when he was struck once more by that foul smell. Grimacing as though from a physical hurt, he opened one of his windows and turned his fan on full before sitting down.

Hoogstratten sat in a chair opposite, his knobbly hands clutching the black briefcase.

"Firstly, Mr. Hoogstratten. My rate is—" What happened next occurred in a merciful blur. Carmichael heard the click as the briefcase was opened, he saw the gun in the man's hand and then it was in his mouth. The trigger was pulled and there was a muffled explosion as the old man's brains splattered over the ceiling.

Bits dripped onto the desk.

Suddenly, as though time had been reversed, Hoogstratten's head reformed, the gaping, bloody exit wound seeming to suck back that which had just been blasted out. There was no mess whatsoever to indicate that a gruesome suicide had just taken place.

The very foundation of Carmichael's sanity rocked. Savagely, he shook his head, bewildered, scared, unable to comprehend that which he had just witnessed. There was a sudden beading of sweat on his forehead and he could feel his pulse racing. Stunned horror flooded through him, almost drowning him in its terror-laden deluge. None of this had happened. It couldn't have.

"I'm sorry that you had to see that, but I think it the surest and quickest way to get you to believe what I'm about to tell you." Hoogstratten rested the smoking revolver on the desk. "There was only the one bullet. But please, take it if it will make you feel better."

Carmichael found himself incapable of speech. He looked to the ceiling, eyes narrowing as he saw the entry hole where the bullet had shot through the plaster. He had just watched as the man seated no more than five feet away had blown his brains out and yet, he was now talking. There was no blood anywhere. How could this be? His only possible explanation was that it had been a bad vision, perhaps something to do with the coffee? He pushed his cup to one side. Or maybe it was the smell. Yes, he thought. That was it. Some kind of hallucinogen.

"I did just shoot myself," verified Hoogstratten as though he had just read the other's mind. "What you saw was real."

Carmichael wasn't buying any of this. He slid the gun over, away from the other's reach. The man was an oddball, of that at least there was no question. "No. Sorry, I—" His hands were trembling now and there was a tightening in his stomach as fear and apprehension contorted into an uncomfortable knot. Gulping, he stared, disbelieving, his eyes glazed, temporarily unseeing. "This isn't happening. It's not—"

"My problem, Mr. Carmichael, is that I can't die," Hoogstratten interrupted, reaching into his briefcase and removing a tightly-bound sheaf of documents. "I have no soul, you see. My parents offered my soul to Satan when I was born. In return for which they no doubt got the usual rewards; wealth, power, good fortune, you name it. It's my belief that I should have received the same on my thirty-third birthday had I not been 'killed' in a traffic accident two weeks ago. The doctors resuscitated me, even though I had technically died. It was during those few minutes when I was 'dead' that my parents' contract was fulfilled and Satan claimed my soul. Now I exist in this living limbo. I'm twenty-nine years of age. I'm ageing, deteriorating, but I know I can't die, something you've just witnessed yourself. Oh, I've tried several times. Jumping from tower blocks, falling into the path of subway trains. Nothing works."

His head clenched in his hands, Carmichael mentally wrestled with the insanity of all of this. Silent screams rang and echoed though his mind and for a moment he wondered whether or not it was *his* brain that had erupted and was now dripping from overhead. It certainly felt that way as he tried to process and comprehend the utter madness that he had seen and that the man opposite was relating. He glanced once more at the bullet hole. That was real, he told himself. Therefore, was it conceivable that Hoogstratten had missed and that he had merely mentally filled in the bloody aftermath by way of what he had anticipated? It was a far-fetched explanation but when faced with the alternative—

"I appreciate it's hard to believe and I assure you I too was unable to accept it for a long time. But it *is* the truth. And in order to prevent me from having to take my life as it were, over and over again, the sooner you come to terms with my status the better. Only then will we be able to proceed to what needs doing."

"Sorry, I'm a bit confused." Carmichael tried to focus, to shake away the unreality of the situation. Everything was still a bit of a blur. "What were you saying?"

"I'm saying, Mr. Carmichael, that I'm incapable of dying."

"Yes, yes. You said something about your soul?" Carmichael coughed and covered his mouth with a hand. His eyes were watering though he knew not why. Maybe it was the smell, which even his fan and the fresh air coming in through the open window had trouble in negating. The man was a nutter. A stinking weirdo. And yet how could he explain what had happened? Simple. It hadn't happened. *But it had*, his tortured mind screamed at him.

"I no longer have a soul. It's my belief that Satan took it from me, believing I had truly died."

Hoogstratten untied the knot fastening his paperwork together. "I have the actual contract here." He flicked through the pile of yellowed documents, news-cuttings and old photographs before taking out a rather rigid sheet of vellum. It was mammal-skin only in this case it was human. The sheet was framed along the borders by numerous dark and unholy sigils and apart from the two signatures, which had been written in blood, the writing on it appeared, to the private investigator at least, to be gibberish.

"Are you telling me that Satan has your soul?"

"Yes, I believe so." Hoogstratten pointed to a part of the bizarre document. "I can't read much of this. However, from what I've managed to piece together I've discovered that should I die before my thirty-third birthday then Satan may take full owner-ship of my soul. It's my belief that my parents, whose signatures I take it are here, thought that they were pulling a fast one on Satan, for they clearly interpreted certain clauses mentioned in the small print below as meaning that I wouldn't die before my thirty-third year, by which time I would be granted all of the benefits they had been given. Technically or rather medically, one could argue that I did die, no matter how briefly, when I was in the crash, so by taking the letter of the law, Satan has managed to—"

"This is absolute nonsense. It's absurd!" Carmichael had to do something in order to prevent this conversation from slid-ing deeper into madness. "None of this makes sense. How can you expect me to believe any of this? You're insane." He now wished he had given the man the brush-off at the entrance and had gone for his train instead. Hoogstratten could keep his money as far as he was concerned. This was one case he could well do without.

"I'll ask for your assistance once more. Please, help me."

"I'm sorry, but this has gone far enough. I want you out of here. Now."

"Very well. You leave me with no alternative." Hoogstratten removed a dark purple gem from his briefcase and held it up in his right hand, his scrawny fingers locked around its edges. The crystalline stone pulsed like a heart in his grip. An inner light, refracted from its countless facets, played within its mysterious depths.

Carmichael found his eyes drawn to the gem. He couldn't look away. It held him. Captivated him. Hypnotised him.

"Believe me, I didn't want to resort to this but you leave me no choice." Hoogstratten began to move the gem in an anti-clockwise motion. "This stone I also found amongst the docu-ments in addition to instructions for its use. So, listen well, Mr. Carmichael. I'm going to give you a man's name and an address. The man's name is Gyorgy Madarasz and from what I've found out he's the one person in Los Angeles who may be able to shed some light on this. The address is one hundred and forty-three

East Street. I want you to find this man. Talk to him about my situation and find out how I can regain my soul."

* * * *

An hour later, Carmichael was in a cab going though the busy city thoroughfares, heading downtown, a black folder clenched in his right hand. This was an area he normally avoided, for crime, drug-use and over population were prevalent, making it perhaps one of the worst man-made environments on the planet, or so he often claimed. There was no denying the fact that it was dangerous and predominantly lawless, a cosmopolitan ghetto in which the street gangs; the Mexicans, the Blacks and the Hispanics all fought and killed for dominance alongside the bosses who ran the slimy criminal underworld.

Gazing out of the cab windows, he found himself taking in the transformation as the wealth, the glitz and the opulence of Los Angeles reverted to the squalor, the strewn litter and the graffiti-ridden streets downtown. The people here were different too. Suspicious-looking crowds gathered on street corners, their eyes ever watchful, unfriendly. Sullen-faced, scrawny individuals, some covered in tattoos, jaywalked or sat slumped on walls, brown paper bags containing cheap booze gripped tightly in their hands.

"What's the address again?" asked the cabbie.

"One hundred and forty-three East Street." Carmichael's response was instantaneous. There was a strange feeling in his mind, a niggling uncertainty as to why exactly he was here. It was something that his brain couldn't exactly explain. That something inexplicable had happened not that long ago in his office he felt sue, but just what, he couldn't fully remember.

The cab driver took a right and slowed down. There was no one around. The place looked dead.

"You thinking of moving here?" chuckled the driver.

"That kind of thing. Are we near?"

"We've just passed ninety-nine, so it's a bit further."

The cab pulled over outside number one hundred and forty-three. It was a three-storey building that looked, like the rest of the street, unfit for habitation. The only thing it did look fit for was the wrecking ball.

Carmichael got out and paid the driver who was only too happy to accelerate off and get away from there. Taking in the sight before him with a critical eye, he shook his head disparagingly and, folder in hand, went up the steps to the main door, a stout-looking thing of polished black, a dragon-headed knocker set at head height. Unlike most of the other doorways there were no visible electronic bell-pushes so he gave a loud rap.

Twenty seconds passed and there was no reply.

Carmichael knocked again.

This time a second-storey window was opened and a bald-headed, tattooed face glared down. "What're you wanting?"

Carmichael stepped back from the door and looked up. "I'm here to see Gyorgy Madarasz."

"Are you a cop?"

"No. I'm not a cop. I've been sent to seek his help."

"Who sent you?"

"Daniel Hoogstratten."

"Hoogstratten? Never heard of him."

"Does that matter? He's sent me to find Madarasz. It's important."

"What's *your* name?"

"Vincent Carmichael."

"All right, I'll be down in a minute." The window was closed.

Carmichael felt uneasy, still trying to comprehend what was going on and just what the circumstances were that had brought him to this place. Fragments of memory were coming back to him now, more so when he had mentioned Hoogstratten's name. Something about the Devil, wasn't it? It was while he was struggling to remember, that the door opened, the individual he had seen at the open window now standing before him. He was even scruffier than his first appearance had suggested. His jeans were ripped and he was bare-chested, a great percentage of his visible skin covered in tattoos.

"Name's Weller. Gyorgy's upstairs. Come in and I'll take you to him."

For a moment, the paranoid, untrusting part of Carmichael that had served him well over the years warned him against following the other. It could be a trap, after all. He could go in and never come out. Things like that happened on a daily basis around here, of that he had no doubt. But then came that unspoken command from elsewhere, instructing him to venture in, to cast aside his wariness and his common sense.

"This way."

Carmichael entered the dingy, unfurnished hallway. There was a smell in the air. It reminded him of incense but as he hadn't been to church in over thirty years it could have been anything. It was no doubt the fumes from some illicit substance or other that some deadbeat was smoking in one of the ground floor rooms.

Climbing a narrow flight of steps they came out onto a squalid landing. The walls here were a riot of terrible spray-painted scenes; man-devouring demons interspersed with pentagrams, warped, melted, open-mouthed faces crying out in silent screams, weird cabbalistic symbols and entire diabolical verses written in numerous languages.

There was something in the dynamic manner in which the garish murals had been painted that fascinated Carmichael, something indefinable that drew his eye at both the religious and the aesthetic level. The vibrant colours portrayed well the violent passion with which the artist or artists had produced this work, which at first glance appeared far more chaotic than it really was. Indeed, it was only with closer examination that some of the more horrifying scenes became fully discernible, such was the almost camouflage ability with which they had been blended into the greater image. In this context, the overall effect was to ensnare the viewer, to drag them into the two-dimensional terror.

It was hard not to be distracted by the bizarre imagery for it was everywhere. In the corridor they were now heading along, even the ceiling and the floor were painted so that Carmichael couldn't help but step on a painted grotesque. For here was a hideous cross between a man and a giant toad, its enormous sloppy tongue wrapped around what appeared to be a struggling cherub. On the wall to his right, at knee level, there was a flaming horned skull, the skill with which it had been done almost giving it a semblance of motion, as though at any time it was about to snap and burn and fly down the corridor.

And then they were at a door. Like the walls, it too was adorned with fiendish art.

Weller knocked.

"Enter."

"Okay, Gyorgy'll see you now. In you go." Weller opened the door and stood aside.

The small room Carmichael entered was dark and shadowy, the curtains drawn tight, the only light coming from a set of flickering black candles that gave off an oleaginous and repellent smell. In the dimness, he could make out a dark figure sat atop a pile of heaped cushions in the corner of the room. The nightmarish illustrations and paintings on the walls seemed to be even more macabre and diabolical in content in here.

"Mr. Carmichael. Weller tells me that you've been sent by a Mr. Hoogstratten," came a sibilant voice.

If someone ever trained a snake how to talk, Carmichael was sure that's how it would sound. He gulped, narrowing his eyes, trying to discern just who or what had spoken.

"That's correct. He's sent me to ask you for help." As if a door had opened in his mind, Carmichael could suddenly remember exactly why he was there. "Seems that Satan's left him without a soul and—"

"And he wants me to get it back for him?" Madarasz shifted his not inconsiderable bulk on the cushions. "Well, why don't you come in and we will see if any re-negotiations can be done? I take it you have the original contract with you?"

"I do." There was a chill feeling of sweat on Carmichael's back and his heart was beginning to thud madly against his ribs. He told himself that there was nothing of which to be afraid, but inwardly, he knew this not to be the case. Some other power was keeping him here, bolstering his will, enabling him to stand his ground in a situation from which a normal man would turn and flee. He doubted whether anyone sane would have chosen to walk along these ghastly-painted corridors, let alone enter this room with its weird occupant. Dragged against his own will, he took several hesitant steps forward.

The door closed behind him.

"Right, let's get down to business. Give me the contract." A fleshy hand reached out from the shadowy corner.

The private investigator opened his folder and removed the unholy vellum sheet. It felt slick and almost wet on his fingertips. He handed it over.

What followed was a lengthy deliberation, a protracted, uncomfortable wait whilst the dark-shrouded Madarasz slowly read the written agreement. At times, Carmichael saw the other nod or shake his head, obviously in agreement or disagreement over certain aspects of the legal writ. Some points clearly had the other puzzled for he paused and scratched his head as though lost in thought.

After a space of about ten minutes it looked as though some kind of conclusion had been reached.

"Well, I haven't seen a contract like this one in quite some time," Madarasz stated. "It's fairly in-depth regarding many of its stipulations. That said, there are one or two things in the lesser articles that may prove advantageous to your client. Now, before we continue, I should inform you that I act purely in an intermediary role. See me as a mediator if you wish. It's my role to act on the part of certain aggrieved parties and to represent them before my Master."

"Satan?"

"Well, that's but one name of many, but I suppose as far as you're concerned it's good enough."

"Can you get this contract reversed? Is it possible for Hoogstratten to regain his soul?"

"Let's not be too hasty," said the man in the shadows. "Yes, admittedly, there are one or two things that strike me as contractual breaches, but alas I think a lot of it will be down solely to interpretation. The most apparent one being; was Mr.

Hoogstratten actually killed? That is, *dead*, when my Master took his soul. There are clear arguments for and against."

"He told me he had been resuscitated after his accident. I think the doctors pronounced him dead and they then brought him back."

"Well, I guess that's the crux of the problem, isn't it? You see, as far as my Master's concerned dead's dead. Hoogstratten did die in the car accident. Yes, I have to admit, my Master's a little behind the times when it comes to the wonders of modern surgery and medicine—in fact, dare I say it, I think He's still stuck somewhat in the Dark Ages; leeches, poultices, willow-herb and all that." Madarasz let out a sigh.

"Look, I don't care much for this legal nonsense. Is it possible to reclaim Hoogstratten's soul or not?"

"Let me look over this once more."

Carmichael waited in the darkness whilst the man seated in the corner—if indeed he was a man—read and re-read the contract. It was a long wait and he began to feel uncomfortable, standing there, not knowing what the outcome would be. Yet again, he felt that inner power strengthening him, empowering him and providing him with the resolve to stay where a normal man would have ran away, screaming. Wisps of memory assaulted his mind, coalescing into firm memories of actuality. He had been hypnotised, sent here against his will; under a spell, a geas. He was being used as nothing more than a puppet by Hoogstratten; dispatched in order to find the means to remove the latter's curse.

Eventually, Madarasz looked up, his eyes tinged crimson in the candlelight. "Right, firstly, you'll be pleased to know that I do believe there's a flaw in this contract which can be exploited by your client. It's not a loophole as such but rather a fundamental misinterpretation which, certainly to my reading of it, does enable Mr. Hoogstratten to challenge the legality of this contract. Not only was he an unwilling participant, his parents being the ones who authorised it, but I think a strong argument could be made to question the terms under which my Master brought about the premature termination, by which I mean the aforementioned car crash in which the plaintiff was 'killed,' for lack of a better term. It's a tricky, onerous case this and I think in order to take this further certain concessions are going to have to be made by both parties. As I said, view me as a mediator. The man in the middle."

"The man in the middle?"

"Yes. Trust me, you wouldn't want to see what I look like when I do work for the 'other side.'"

"I'm not sure we're any nearer to helping my client. I ask once again, is it possible for Hoogstratten to reclaim his soul? He's not got much time left. He ageing terribly and there's a dreadful stink coming from him."

"Don't worry about the smell. Every living being would smell such if their soul were to become detached. As for the rapidity of his ageing, I'm afraid that's to be expected. Devoid of his soul, Hoogstratten will continue to deteriorate until the point where his mortal presence decays. His flesh and his bones will disintegrate into nothing but his presence will remain. Without his soul, he will forever haunt this world you know. The very thought makes one shudder."

"You mentioned concessions? I take it that you're in contact with Satan so can you tell me here and now what these 'concessions' entail?"

"No, I will need to see your client. I can understand that he was hesitant about coming here but I can assure you that it is safe. He has nothing to fear, at least not from me."

* * * *

Only a day had passed and yet Hoogstratten looked noticeably worse, his hair now showing flecks of white amidst the tangled grey and the odour that emanated from him was wince-making. Carmichael was torn between anger at the way he was being used and extreme pity for the man's plight. Madarasz was as unsettling as the first time Carmichael had seen him and Hoogstratten was trembling slightly in his chair.

"Well, Mr. Hoogstratten. The first question I must ask you is this, did you know about the contract before your 'death'?" Madarasz stared fixedly at the plaintiff.

"Not a thing, I knew nothing about my true parents, believing them to have been killed in a house fire when I was a baby. Two weeks ago, after I left hospital, I knew things weren't right. My injuries, although life-threatening, healed miraculously. I felt drained, empty and then the aging started, followed by the nightmares. It was the nightmares that led me to the old ancestral family home, a place I'd never visited before, never even knew existed. It's a ruin now. Yet, in the attic, hidden in a fireplace, I found the contract and the other documents. No doubt they were meant to have been destroyed but never were." Hoogstratten suddenly hurled the briefcase to the floor. "How can I be bought and sold like this! Is my soul not my own property?"

Madarasz looked steadily at the man before him. "That is the crux of the matter. That and the manner of your death. Now, I've been in communication with a representative for my Master, and whilst He is somewhat preoccupied with something else at the moment, I've been informed that He is prepared to take certain rulings into consideration in order to reach an agreeable solution. I do think it's in everyone's interest to reach a compromise. Now you clearly hold to the stance that you've been robbed of your soul despite being an innocent party and that as it states in the contract your soul was to remain yours until your death and that death itself is the point of contention, my Master is willing to make an offer."

"What kind of offer? No, let me guess. Satan wants me to murder my parents if I could ever find them or perhaps burn down all of the churches in the city, yes?"

"No, nothing of the sort. It's my Master's belief that you have in your possession something that once belonged to Him. A stone with incredible powers. I take it you know of it?"

Carmichael certainly knew of it. It had to be the one Hoogstratten had hypnotised him with.

"*That's it?* All I have to do is relinquish that accursed stone? I'll willingly—"

"Not quite." Madarasz brought his hands together as though in prayer, interlocking his fingers. "There's one small proviso."

"And what's that?" asked both Hoogstratten and Carmichael simultaneously.

"As a gesture of your goodwill, my Master would like it returned to Him in person."

* * * *

Through the demonic power of the stone, Hoogstratten forced Carmichael to go in his stead; to be the agent to return the foul thing to Satan. Now, as he stood facing one particular stretch of hideously painted wall in Madarasz's house, the private investigator felt an inner urge trying to battle the compulsion that was forcing him onwards. The torture in his mind threatened at any moment to pull him apart and it felt as though there was a raging fire inside him.

On his right, impassive, Hoogstratten waited. In one hand he held the purple gem. In the other, he held the contract that he hoped Satan was going to invalidate.

Madarasz began reading the writing, the incantation that was on the wall. It was a language unlike anything either of the other two had ever heard before, the reader's intoned words more like snarls and hisses; terrible sounds that sent a chill through those that heard them; obscene phonetics that were not meant to be uttered by a human voice.

And then, before their eyes, the infernal images began to shimmer and become animate. Hellish, bipedal, pig-like beasts snorted and paraded; small, writhing bodies skewered on the terrible pitchforks they wielded. Flames erupted throughout the length of the corridor and melting faces screamed and bubbled, blood pouring from their eyes. Pentagrams flickered and vanished, replaced with patches of utter darkness, nebulous voids in which tenebrous, amorphous shapes laughed and slithered.

Had it not been for the power of the stone, Carmichael would have certainly gone incurably insane, reduced to a blubbering wreck. As it was, he merely stared, eyes wide, mercifully incapable of taking in the entirety of the demonic phantasmagoria that was unfolding, yelling and burning all around him.

Suddenly, a door-shaped, black rectangle appeared in the midst of the demon-filled diorama.

Madarasz gestured towards it.

Hoogstratten handed over the gem and the contract to Carmichael, who, with a deep breath stepped into the darkness.

* * * *

Reality vanished and Carmichael shivered in the freezing cold, narrowing his eyes to mere slits in an effort to shield them from the sudden glare of whiteness. Before him, stretched mile upon mile of broken glacial land; an alien world of shattered cliffs, ice-scoured rocks, deep crevasses and, in the far distance, a dark and threatening mountain range that spanned the horizon. But it was the sky overhead that filled him with the most terror, for it was an obscene clash of vibrant red, orange and purple colours, an infernal aurora that had been sliced open, spilling blood from its chaotic insides.

A sudden blizzard struck at him without mercy, icy fingers grasping and clawing sadistically.

Carmichael turned and was somewhat relieved to see that the shimmering black portal was still at his back. Hopefully it provided a means of return. Staring into the frozen wilderness, he tried to discern anything, a landmark to head towards.

There was nothing. The isolation was a terror beyond imagination, beyond nightmare. He wanted to scream and scream, and it was only through the power of the stone that he managed to refrain from doing so. Shoes crunching on the thin layer of snow, he willed himself forward, taking small steps, his eyes trying to see in the partial whiteout as the snow continued to gust and eddy all around him. Head down, he walked, not knowing where he was or where he was going until, within a relatively short time, the snow cleared and he found himself able to see further. He continued on through the icy waste for how long he did not know. Time itself here was warped if indeed it existed at all. There was pain in his feet and his face and fingers felt as though they had become frostbitten by the time he came to the edge of the great crevasse and looked down.

The sight that lay below paralysed him with horror.

There, some three hundred feet down, at the base of the glacial rift, was the remains of a massive carcass of something or other; a dead, practically skeletal, curved-tusked and horned creature, its remains half-buried in the snow, the ice and the rock. If what Carmichael was looking at had once truly been a living thing then it would have been gargantuan in scale, dwarfing the countless high tors and pinnacles with ease. There was something about it that made him think of preserved woolly mammoths but obviously this was something much, much bigger; mind-shatteringly colossal.

Carmichael stared in awe, half-expecting the monstrous sight before him to melt away as though it were a mirage brought on by exhaustion and fear, but the thing remained, mocking him with its refusal to disappear. In stunned amazement, he continued to look, noting the hideous shreds of gore and desiccated flesh, the unscavenged scraps, which hung to the bones. A huge span of leathery, ragged skin stretched tightly across parts of the enormous ribcage, forming some kind of crude covering. Flaps of preserved, frozen meat still clung to a giant, protruding leg and cloven hoof which, due to its raised angle, gave the thing the appearance of dynamism, almost as though it were about to haul itself up in order to once again rampage across the land. Its eye-sockets were empty and cavernous; dark holes within the scoured, gleaming white bone. There was a rawness to the thing which bizarrely juxtaposed an overall impression of timeless death.

Over to his left, he was relieved to see that a worn and tortuous-looking flight of narrow steps had been hewn into the cliff-face, permitting a relatively easy means of descent. The wind grew in strength and began howling at him, buffeting him, and yet, despite the dreadful conditions, he succeeded in reaching the bottom of the huge chasm.

The frozen ground was cracked wide by gaping fissures that zigzagged like crazy lightning across the ice-blasted ground.

Looking down one such crevasse, Carmichael saw that it fell away into the depths; small, barred, cell-like openings visible halfway down, set into the chasm walls. Peering hard, he thought he could make out ledges, whether natural or otherwise, on which some form of primordial, grisly totem poles had been erected. Shaking his head, he made for the ossified ruins.

The going was hard, the presence of the ravines often causing him to have to backtrack and retrace his steps. Like some infuriating maze, the ragged rifts in the ground seemed almost intentionally laid out, forcing him further from what he had to assume was his goal. He would get near, certain that this time he would be able to reach the grisly, titanic stronghold, only to find that he had to go further out, and once more make his way inwards. There was only one true approach, the numerous other routes leading to abrupt cliff edges. Yet slowly, patiently, and more importantly, driven by the gem he now held aloft, Carmichael picked his way through the hellish labyrinth, until, there before him, reared the giant, open, fanged maw; the entrance to Satan's demesne.

Stiffly, Carmichael walked up to the massive skull. A terrible stench emanated from beyond almost as though it was a rancid breath exhaled from somewhere within. The fearsome upper and lower mandibles were ridged with rows and rows of fangs and, although open wide, gave the uncomfortable impression that at any moment they would clamp down in a savage gnash that would rend any trespasser to a bloody morsel fit for devouring.

There was only darkness beyond.

The steely determination granted by the gem overcame the paralysing fear and drove him forward, into that dark opening. The dark and the cold were pervasive, enveloping, threatening, as was the strong sensation that by crossing that terrible threshold all hope of return had now gone.

* * * *

Carmichael screamed, covered his ears and closed his eyes as clashing sounds and colours collided and dark things in the purple mists reached out and sought to snatch him. The gem he held pulsated its terrible light, illuminating him in a protective effulgence that kept these terrors of the Pit at bay, making *them* recoil in fear. Monstrous, scaled, serpentine abominations slithered before him as many-legged things scurried amongst the shadows, weaving giant webs that dripped blood from the countless ensnared bodies, some of which had been wrapped up and were now no more than horrible husks.

Pushing his way past these demonic horrors, Carmichael soon found himself at a set of immense double doors carved from black stone. The portals swung open as he neared and raised the strange gem.

And then he was in an immense throne room, a hideously fiendish place filled with the malign and the ugly, the violent and the malicious, the dark and the monstrous. For this was Satan's court and the Lord of Hell Himself was seated on an enormous black, skull-bedecked throne on a raised dais at the opposite end.

Carmichael saw many things in that chamber; things that very few mortals were ever meant to see.

Satan chose to appear in His most common guise when on this plane of existence—that of a fearsome horned monster; thirteen feet tall, gaunt, green-skinned, limbs elongated. In places, His skin was painted with black and red markings, giving Him the appearance of a living, raw skeleton. He was dressed resplendently in a full black robe that scintillated and flickered as skull-like faces bubbled to the surface and then vanished. One foot was cloven, the other encased within a massive iron boot. The crown on His head was exquisite in its brilliance. In one hand, He grasped a huge intricately-carved sceptre, its length intertwined with living snakes.

The grotesque gathering parted, allowing Carmichael audience with The Dark One.

"You have my stone," Satan boomed, His voice echoing around the many-pillared throne room. "Give it to me."

"Only when you rescind this contract and swear to grant me safe passage away from here, back to whence I came."

Carmichael could feel the terrible presence of those foul things in the room as they began to gather and press around him. He could also sense the evil that Satan was directing straight at him, the Devil's eyes boring into him with a potent lethality. Without the stone, he was well aware that he would be powerless to stop the demons from tearing him apart or worse.

"You have my word."

"And how sincere is that? After all, how do I know that once I hand it over you won't renege on the deal? Similarly, how do I know that without the stone I won't be killed outright with the insanity of all this?"

"The answer is simple. You don't." Something resembling a wicked smile creased Satan's face. A clawed hand reached out. "Hand it over."

"Hoogstratten regains his soul? And I get out?"

"My, what an untrusting soul. Maybe you'd care to join my collection?" Satan pointed towards a vast archway, beyond which was another room. In the centre was a large tank filled with a pea-soup-like jellified mass in which thousands of tortured faces ballooned and attempted to break free. "The soul of Daniel Hoogstratten is one of those held within. You give me the stone and I will see that the two are reunited once more."

"Very well, agreed. After all, it's what I've been sent here to do." Reluctantly, Carmichael handed the stone over and then darkness engulfed him.

* * * *

"Where am I? I can't see!"

Madarasz was shaking him. "Steady. Your vision will right itself in a minute or so. You're back in my house in Los Angeles."

Carmichael was shuddering violently. Blurry images swam drunkenly in his spinning mind before assuming definition and form. He was sat against a wall in one of the horribly-painted corridors. He could feel the blood coursing through his veins and there was a dreadful pounding at his temples.

"You can consider yourself most fortunate, for my Master is not often so generous as to enable one to return having seen what you've no doubt seen. Consider yourself...*blessed*." Madarasz chuckled to himself, an evil-sounding, gurgling noise that came from the depths of his pendulous belly.

Wearily, Carmichael pulled himself to his feet. His bones ached and he felt as though a thousand red-hot pins were prickling the flesh on his back. His vision swam once more before he steadied himself, using the wall for support even though he was reluctant to touch it.

"No doubt you're wondering where Mr. Hoogstratten is," said Madarasz. "Well, you'll be pleased to know that my Master, in his sublime generosity, has re-acquainted him with his soul. There was only one small detail that wasn't quite to your client's liking and that was—"

"*What?* Tell me!"

"Well, simply that my Master has re-acquainted him with his soul by taking him to Hell where he will spend an eternity of torture. I daresay you were shown the vat in which my Master keeps souls—"

"Cheating son of a bitch! That's not what was promised!"

"I think you'll find that it was according to the letter of the agreement, if not the spirit. Now, you should be leaving, Mr. Carmichael. I'll show you the way out. For your sake, I would suggest that you don't return."

THE SONS OF SET-PERIBSEN

*It is said that all men fear time—but time
surely feared the Sons of Set-Peribsen...*

Accompanied by a bustling hum of discussion and the shuffling of many feet, the large lecture hall slowly emptied, the one and a half hour talk and the questions that had followed now over. The chamber could normally seat two hundred but such had been the interest that the numbers inside had swelled to nearer three hundred, with many students, academics and curious members of the public resorting to sitting or standing in the aisles, all eager to hear, first-hand, of Professor Sidney Emerson's doomed expedition. That the esteemed Egyptologist had been the sole survivor of that ill-fated mission was common knowledge, having been widely reported in the media, but this was the first time since returning from Egypt, four months previously, that he had given a public account of what had actually happened.

And yet, 'Wolf' Jackson, ex-Eighth Army soldier, adventurer, treasure-hunter and dealer in ill-gotten antiquities was convinced that the professor had not given the full story, providing his listeners with only the edited version. For he was in possession of certain facts that told a different tale, a story much darker than the one the elderly Emerson had just related. He believed he knew just why the professor had glossed over the more implausible elements of the account. After all, the old academic had a reputation to maintain and if even half of what Jackson suspected was true then it would be the last thing anyone in their right mind would want to publicly declare.

Consequently, Jackson had sat and listened, bored for the main part, as for ninety minutes or so Emerson had instead focused on the background leading up to the expedition. Talking with measured clarity about how the necessary funding had been obtained from the Egypt Exploration Society and how, with a team of ten research assistants comprised of archaeologists, Egyptologists and geologists, they had set off into the rugged, blisteringly-hot, desert wilderness of Sinai aboard three specially adapted, all-terrain jeeps.

They had been well prepared; equipped and outfitted with all manner of essentials for ten days of hard desert exploration. Initial work had been carried out at the Middle Kingdom temple to the goddess Hathor at Serabit el-Khadim, recording many of the stelae and drawing detailed plans of the site. Using this as a base, they had then sent out a surveying group in one of the jeeps to see if they could locate any hitherto undiscovered petroglyphs or quarry locations. When the group had failed to return by nightfall, Emerson had sent out a radio message to the expedition's headquarters based in Cairo. Rebuffed and informed to sit tight in the belief that the missing would in all likelihood return in the morning, the professor, as expedition leader, decided to do just that.

The remainder of the story had been drastically edited, at least as far as Jackson was concerned, for Emerson picked up the account two days later when he had found himself, alone in a hospital bed in Suez; wracked by pain, burned red-black by the sun and close to death from dehydration. Apparently he had been brought there by the headman from a tribe of local Bedouin who had found him wandering aimlessly and muttering strange things. At this point, Emerson had admitted, rather embarrassedly, that he didn't know what had happened during those two days he had been in the desert, saying only that sunstroke, lack of water and complete disorientation had profoundly affected him. In hospital, it was found that he had been bitten by a snake, possibly a horned viper, the venom from which undoubtedly contributed to his overall sense of delirium.

He had no recollection whatsoever of what had happened at the camp but the harsh fact was that although two of the wrecked jeeps had been found there was no trace of any of the other members of the team. It had been news that had shocked and confounded many and not just in the archaeological world. Although the Egyptian authorities had been quick to respond, believing that a renegade splinter Bedouin faction might be responsible, no one was ever held accountable for the disappearances.

Jackson waited until the last of the hangers-on—those irksome lecture-goers who always want to prise some last titbit of information out of the speaker—had cleared off, before making his way down the aisle to the stage, where the professor was busy putting his slides and notes away.

Emerson saw him approaching. He looked up through his circular spectacles, eyes narrowing in uncertain recognition. His face hardened.

"Professor Emerson," acknowledged Jackson, smiling. "You might have heard of me. The name's—"

"I know you," replied the professor, acerbically. "You're that tomb-robber, aren't you? I sincerely hope I've not given you any ideas about where to plunder any more archaeological sites. It's people like you that give archaeology a bad name. If I had my way I'd have you arrested. I know of certain members in the Egyptian Antiquities Council who would be only too pleased to see you behind bars."

Jackson shrugged and offered the other a cheery grin. "I see my reputation precedes me once again."

"Well I've no time for the likes of you." Emerson snapped shut his briefcase. "So, if you'll excuse me—"

"Hold on a moment." Jackson made to block the professor. "It could be that I've got something that might interest you. A certain little thing that I found in the desert, perhaps."

Emerson stared fixedly at the treasure-hunter. "What are you talking about?"

"It just so happens that I've done some of my own investigations into the disappearance of your expedition." Jackson reached into a jacket pocket and took out a wrap of soft leather. This he unfolded, removing a palm-sized piece of inscribed rock. "As you know, I'm no academic, but I do recognise the name of Set-Peribsen." He handed it over.

Emerson's eyes widened as he studied the hieroglyphics on the stone. It did indeed show the name of the Second Dynasty pharaoh, the *serekh*—the rectangular motif used for containing the monarch's name—surmounted by the Set figure as opposed to the hawk of Horus. It had to be nearly five thousand years old.

"Where did you find this? Abydos? Saqqara?"

"Neither. I found this close to Serabit el-Khadim."

"But that's a Middle Kingdom temple. Chronologically speaking, almost a thousand years separates the two."

"I said *close* to. Some fifteen miles south of there, in the middle of nowhere, there's a series of rock-cut tombs. Very few know of their existence. I think they may have been built to house the dead from the nearby turquoise mines at Wadi Maghara, but I'm not entirely sure, nor have I ever been inside them."

"But the evidence we have suggests that it was not until the reign of Djoser, in the Third Dynasty, that those mines were put into operation."

"Seems that view now has to be questioned."

Emerson studied the stone. It intrigued him, largely due to the mention of the name, Set-Peribsen, and its alleged provenance. The history of the Archaic Period—the First and Second Dynasties—had always been his main focus of research and during that phase of Egyptian history, despite the paucity of written evidence, one main religious event stood out, one that had perplexed scholars. For it was during the rule of Set-Peribsen, whom some experts identified as Sekhemib, that a radical new theology had appeared with the veneration of Set—the god of the desert, foreigners and later associated with the power of evil—as opposed to that of Horus. Like Amenhotep IV, later Akhenaten of the Eighteenth Dynasty, he erased his original name on the funerary stelae erected at his tomb in the Umm el-Qaab at Abydos, replacing it with his newly acquired Set name. He had been the first historically recorded heretic.

"I see you're interested in my little find."

Emerson handed the stone back. "Well, it appears authentic. There have been a lot of similar objects turn up on the black market as I'm sure *you* know. Not all of them are genuine. However, I do believe this to be the real thing and as a consequence I am somewhat puzzled as to why you found it where you did. I'm also interested in these rock-cut tombs you mention. Although I think they will belong to much later Old Kingdom interments they are certainly worth investigating."

"Excellent. That being the case, I was wondering whether you'd be willing to accompany me and some of my associates—"

"*Accompany you?* You must be joking." Emerson shook his head. "Can you imagine what that would do for my reputation? Why, you're seen in academic circles as nothing more than a thief, a grave-robber. Why on earth would I team up with you and your band of no-good desperados?"

"Perhaps because I know where these tombs are and you don't. You could spend the next ten years scouring the Sinai looking for them and still not find them. Additionally, I know a little more about the disappearance of your expedition than you do yourself. I have my contacts, you see, in some of the worst areas of Cairo, Alexandria and Suez and if what I've pieced together so far has any basis in reality then believe me I need someone of your experience and expertise on my side." He paused, looking intently at Emerson. "And if I'm right, you need someone with my special skills on your side."

The professor frowned. "You say you know more about the disappearances. I take it that you've gone to the authorities with this information?"

"I have. They weren't interested. To be honest, I don't think they believed me. Besides, I couldn't disclose everything as I don't have the full facts myself yet." Jackson put the stone back in his pocket. "I feel I have little option but to confide in you, and trust me it's not something I normally do. In my line of business trust in others is rare."

"I don't really know what exactly it is you're getting at."

Jackson looked about him, making sure there was no one else in earshot. Apart from the two of them the lecture hall was empty. "Then I guess I'll just have to come straight out with it and ask you: Have you ever heard of the Sons of Set-Peribsen?"

"The *what?*"

"I'll take that as a no. Well, the Sons of Set-Peribsen are a relatively new organisation, and yet one whose members believe they can trace their origins back to the third millennium BC. They're formed largely of occultists and fanatics, but they also have some of the big hitters too; lawyers, bankers and politicians. You know, the worst of society." Jackson gave a wry smile. "They're a secret cult whose aims are to bring about social and religious change; to reinstate a new world order based on anarchy, to sow the seeds of disorder and chaos. One that seeks to overthrow the established governments of the world and thus usher in a time of strife and global revolution. You can obviously see why a dark brotherhood would be thus named."

Emerson shook his head in disbelief. "I've never heard of them and, to be honest, I think you're just making this up. I can see now why the authorities wouldn't believe you. You're mad. I mean, where is the evidence to back up your theories pertaining to this cult? And who exactly are its members? And, even if I were to believe that they do exist are you implying that they were responsible for the disappearance of my expedition party?"

Jackson was about to answer when a side door opened and two men came into view. They were both dressed in long dark coats but that is where all similarity ended, for they were a mismatched pair; one short and dumpy, the other tall and gaunt. There was a reek of menace about them that he didn't like and he silently cursed the fact that he had not got his gun on him— but, he had not expected any intervention so soon.

"Professor Emerson. You must come with us," called out the fat man, his words strangely accented, clearly not English. He reached into a coat pocket and removed a revolver. He raised the gun and pointed it directly at Jackson then without a moment's hesitation pulled the trigger.

The bullet cracked into the wooden podium as Jackson leapt to one side. A second, and then a third shot whistled over his head.

The fat man was coming closer.

Emerson was in stunned shock, his eyes wide and staring, his hands trembling, unable as yet to take in just what was happening. For a moment he was paralysed with fear, incapable of running for safety even though his brain was screaming at his body to do so.

Crouching behind the podium, Jackson knew he was in deep trouble. He had been in worse situations, pinned down by enemy fire in the slums of cities all over the Middle East and North Africa but he at least had usually been armed at the time, able to shoot back. Now he was weaponless and the plump, greasy-faced assassin was almost upon him. Even if he were to make a dash for it, in all likelihood he would only succeed in getting a bullet in the back. And that was something he would never do, much preferring to face his death with a defiant snarl.

Suddenly Emerson found his voice and he began shouting, desperately hoping that someone would come to their rescue. The tall man had him in an arm-lock and was pulling him away.

Now within ten feet from Jackson, the other man decided to put a bullet in the podium, hoping that it would penetrate and hit his target.

Fortunately for Jackson it was made of solid oak and he was unharmed.

When the fat man stepped around it, he doubted whether he'd be as lucky. However, luck—that strange power which, not entrusting his fate to any conventional deity had governed most of his life—was once more on his side. The gunman pulled the trigger, and with an audible click the revolver jammed.

Reaching into his pocket, Jackson removed the rock and threw it with all of his strength straight at the man. His aim was excellent—although admittedly he was more accustomed to throwing hand-grenades, sticks of dynamite and the occasional knife—and the rock struck his target right between the eyes.

Blood streamed from the fat man's forehead and he fell to his knees, cursing. He dropped the gun and brought his hands to his face, blood leaking from between his fingers.

Rushing over, Jackson grabbed him in a vicious headlock and twisted, snapping his neck. Bending down, he picked up the dropped gun and ran after the professor and his captor. The tall man saw the gun in his hand and chose to make a break for it, not knowing that it had jammed. Throwing Emerson to the ground, he ran in long, loping strides towards an emergency exit whereupon he threw the door wide and rushed out into the back streets behind the lecture hall, clearly aware that he and his accomplice had failed in their attempted abduction.

"Are you alright, professor?" asked Jackson, helping the elderly Egyptologist to his feet. He was in two minds about giving chase and going after the gangly assailant.

"Yes, I think so." Clearly shocked and confused, Emerson shook his head, trying to focus, to restore clarity. "Who were those men? I've never seen them before in my life."

"Nor have I, but I can guess who they work for." Jackson walked over to where the fat man's body lay. For a brief moment he regretted having killed him, knowing that there was now no means of interrogating him in order to extract information—information that could prove crucial. Crouching down, he examined the dead man's right hand and loosened a gold ring from his middle finger. The design on it was the same as on the stone which he retrieved and returned to his pocket—the serekh of Set-Peribsen. He began going through the man's pockets, removing a crumpled sheet of notepaper. On it, written in black ink were two lines of Egyptian hieroglyphics.

"Do you think we should call the police?"

"No, not yet." Jackson got to his feet. "He was an agent of the Sons of Set-Peribsen. Here, take a look." He handed over the ring and the piece of paper. "What do you make of this?"

"Well the ring clearly has the name Set-Peribsen, contained within its serekh and with the Set symbol above it." Relieved to have something familiar to focus his mind on, Emerson turned his attention to the hieroglyphics. He frowned and his lips puckered. "Whilst most of it is disjointed and simply wrong, clearly written by, or possibly for, someone with only a very basic grasp of Ancient Egyptian grammar, it would appear to be an order given by someone referred to as The Grand Ipsissimus, 'The Dark Hand of Set,' for my capture."

"'The Dark Hand of Set.' Hmm. I wonder who that could be."

"Hang on a minute." Emerson's eyes widened. "I think I know this writing style—the way in which some of the symbols have been drawn, even the mistakes. After all, I taught him how to read and write hieroglyphics. It's Doctor Stourbridge's work. I'm sure of it."

"Doctor Stourbridge?"

"Yes. He's the curator for the Ancient Egyptian Department at the Museum. But why on earth would he be involved with anything like this? I've known him for years."

"Maybe you don't know him as well as you think."

Emerson wearily rubbed his forehead. "Well what should I, or should I say we, do now? There's a dead man here. Surely we have to inform the police."

"Yes, let's go. You do the talking. They're more likely to believe a man of your standing. Just give them the bare minimum, try and make them believe that your attackers were merely deranged psychos. The least said about their true identity and intent the better—it would only serve to complicate matters. Besides, do you think they'd believe you? In addition, there could well be members of the cult operating at various levels within the police. Once we've done that and assuming we're not imprisoned for murder, I think we should pay this Doctor Stourbridge a visit."

* * * *

It was not until late afternoon the following day that the police decided to drop all charges against Jackson, accepting that he had acted in self-defence and that he had undoubtedly saved the professor's life. The fat man's fingerprints on the gun, and the bullets in the podium supported their story. Jackson's negative reputation had not endeared him to the police superintendent who had repeatedly questioned him and his last words as Jackson left the station was that they would be 'keeping an eye on him.' He was now thankful that he had managed to come out of that little encounter without using his gun, well aware that it would have seriously affected the outcome. As it was he was left wishing he was back on home territory—in the lawless, inhospitable badlands and deserts—where things were much simpler, where he could and had, gunned down his attackers with impunity. But such things would clearly not do for London, he reflected, with a sigh.

He had phoned Emerson and the other remained uncertain and unwilling to get involved any deeper than he already was. Nevertheless, he had agreed to meet up in order to pay Doctor Stourbridge a visit. At Jackson's recommendation, the professor had rented a room in a hotel a mile or so away from his house and had not been back to his office, phoning his university, claiming quite legitimately, that he was still suffering from shock.

They met up at four o'clock and shared a taxi to the Museum. The streets were busy as London always is, tourists and pedestrians thronging all around. The sounds of the traffic was almost deafening as frustrated drivers blared and tooted their horns striving to get through the gridlocked streets. Suicidal cyclists weaved in and out of the cars and buses. Under ideal conditions the journey to the Museum would have taken perhaps fifteen minutes—on this occasion however it took nearly three times as long and Emerson began to wonder whether Stourbridge would still be there.

Eventually they arrived.

"So the police gave you quite a grilling, did they?" Emerson enquired as they stood outside the Museum, the grandiose outer entrance standing at the top of a wide stepped concourse, its sides flanked by huge stone lions.

"And then some. Guess I've just got one of those faces that screams 'guilty.'"

"Yes. I suppose they saved the third-degree treatment for you. I think they realized that whereas I was, and indeed remain, genuinely scared by what happened, you just seemed to take it all in your stride."

"When you've dodged as many bullets as I have and you've got half that number of scars from knife attacks, I guess you get used to it. It was the only way I managed to survive in the Army. I served in the Special Forces under Monty at El-Alamien, being one of only a handful of British units that dared venture into the Qattara Depression in order to carry out secret reconnaissance missions on Rommel's boys. After the war, I just decided to stay in Egypt. After all, there was nothing for me back here. Decided to hire out my services as a mercenary, then as a bodyguard to some of the teams of archaeologists working in Upper Egypt and Nubia. We both like history, professor. The only difference is that I like portable history that has a good market value." Jackson grinned. "I teamed up with some of my old mates for a little bit of fun in Port Said and Suez a couple of years back. That was good."

"Regarding this brotherhood. These Sons—"

"Shh." Jackson brought his finger to his lips, signalling to Emerson to be silent. "Not so loud. One never knows where their members are. It's always best to be cautious. We'll talk more in private."

"Very well. Follow me." Knowing the layout of the Museum rather better than the back of his hand, Emerson led the way. It did not take him long to reach Stourbridge's office. He knocked on the door.

There was no answer.

"Hmm. It would appear that Stourbridge is out. With hind-sight, maybe it would have been better if we'd given him a call to let him know that we were coming."

"So that he could make good his getaway? Or even worse, give him time to lay a trap for us. No, I think not." Jackson tried the door handle and found the door locked. "I think this Stourbridge character may still be unaware that we know of his involvement. The longer we can keep it that way, the better. In the meantime, I think we should see if we can find anything of interest inside." He gave a quick glance around. Noting no one else apart from the professor, he stepped back and gave the door a solid kick with the base of his right boot. The door smashed open.

Emerson stared in shocked disbelief at the other's act of wanton vandalism.

Unbothered, Jackson purposefully strode inside, indicating for Emerson to follow. Once they had both entered, he shut the door behind them and started to take a look around.

The office was fairly small and surprisingly tidy and orderly. There were several books on the shelves. Two large maps of Egypt—one modern, the other perhaps a hundred years old adorned one wall. There was a glass cabinet in which were housed numerous Ancient Egyptian items; canopic jars, roles of papyri, *shabti*-figurines, carved schist palettes, small limestone maceheads and over a dozen pottery vessels of varying sizes and styles. The main desk was likewise covered with well-stacked books, scrolls and several bound ledgers and artefact catalogues.

Removing a screwdriver from an inner jacket pocket, Jackson began opening the locked drawers of Stourbridge's desk. The first two he opened contained nothing of any real interest, but in the bottom one he jemmied open there was a thick black book, the Set-Peribsen motif emblazoned on the cover in gold. The book turned out to be hollow, the cavity inside housing a rolled-up map and a diary.

Jackson passed the map to Emerson. He then consulted the diary, flicking to the last few entries to see if there was anything of note. The diary did indeed confirm Stourbridge's involvement with the Sons of Set-Peribsen for he wrote openly of his attendance at numerous meetings. Most of it was hard to decipher for the handwriting bordered on the illegible.

Emerson unrolled the map. It was fairly sketchy and badly drawn and consequently it took a few moments for him to identify where it represented, the toponymic details leaving much to be desired. It was somewhere in the central Sinai but without any clear reference points. A large 'X' had been marked at one point.

"Let me have a look at the map," said Jackson, taking it from the professor. He studied it briefly. Running his hand down his stubble-covered chin, he then tapped the 'X.' This is very close to where those rock-cut tombs I told you about are located. Could be it's the same place."

"Does the diary reveal anything?" asked Emerson.

"It reveals Stourbridge's connection to the cult. But I can't read most of it. Maybe you can."

Emerson began skimming through the diary. Most of what he could discern was fairly insignificant but from what he could make out, Stourbridge wasn't 'The Dark Hand of Set' for that epithet seemed connected with a certain Ibrahim Bashakti, someone he had never heard of. There was mention of an address, a country manor some thirty-five miles away in Kent, near Ashford. And from the last entry in the diary it would appear that the Sons of Set-Peribsen were holding an important meeting there in a few days time...

* * * *

It was approaching nightfall.

Spying on those going into the large mansion with his binoculars from the branches of a large oak tree that extended over the outer wall, Jackson found himself reflecting on the nature of his own personal involvement against the sinister secret organisation. He had first heard of them during his time in the Eighth Army, when a friend of his had been found murdered in a back alley in the Old Quarter of Cairo, the sign of the Brotherhood carved into her forehead. His friend, with whom he had been romantically involved, had been a young Egyptian woman, a researcher at the Cairo Museum, one who had no doubt stumbled upon something incriminating and as such she had been silenced. Thus had begun his intense loathing of them—an almost holy crusade undertaken with the sole intent of finding them and, if he could, eradicating them. They had proven themselves ruthless and he had no doubt that it was they who had attacked and in all likelihood killed those members of Emerson's expedition.

How the old professor himself had escaped Jackson didn't know. He had questioned Emerson further about the missing two days but the elderly man genuinely couldn't remember. Perhaps it was just pure luck—something that he himself seemed blessed with an inordinate amount of. Perhaps another agency had been responsible. Whatever the case, the Egyptologist was fortunate to be alive.

It was now approaching twilight and so far he had seen almost two dozen different people enter the mansion. If there was a fight then the odds were clearly not stacked in his favour and he regretted that none of his colleagues were here. Not that he had intended on resorting to physical violence but he would have felt far more comfortable knowing that he had the back-up if things did turn nasty, and knowing the Sons of Set-Peribsen as he did, they could well do so. He had his gun and he knew how to use it, a fact that provided some level of reassurance. However, his main mission here was purely reconnaissance—to try and establish what the cult's motives and numbers were and to see whether he could discover any more evidence pertaining to this mysterious site marked in the Sinai desert.

Emerson had chosen, at Jackson's recommendation, not to attend this subterfuge mission. He was an elderly academic after all, not one equipped or trained in such things. Far better that he remained at his secret address where he could pore over his books, trying to throw some light on what was happening and to see if he could discover anything about the location marked on the map. Theirs was unquestionably an odd alliance, forged of complete opposites, but they were stalking the same prey.

Checking that his gun was loaded, Jackson climbed down from the tree. Like a stalking tiger, he crept forward, skirting a low wall and making his way to the house. Shadows clung to the place and a few lights now came on in downstairs rooms. He could see dark forms silhouetted against the windows.

Jackson's pulse was racing—not with fear, but with the thrill of it all. He welcomed the flood of adrenaline, embracing the inherent danger. Pulling up against the nearby wall, he stealthily drew himself into the inky shadows, becoming invisible. He could hear voices coming from inside and he noticed that one of the windows was half-open. The voices were talking quite excitedly and yet the topic of conversation was relatively banal and unimportant, at least as far as he was concerned, dealing as it did with the plummeting financial markets in the United States.

There was more talking followed by a burst of laughter and then a door shut.

Jackson timed two minutes of silence before peering inside. The room was now empty. He waited a few minutes more before raising the window and stealthily climbing inside.

The room was large, high-ceilinged and well furnished. Directly opposite him was a door. There was nothing of noticeable interest in the room, so Jackson walked over to the door. After listening at it and detecting nothing, he gently pushed it open and peered out into the corridor beyond. There was no one to be seen. Quietly, eyes scanning both ends of the corridor, checking to make sure that there wasn't anyone about, he exited the room. Dimly, he became aware of a sound; a low murmuring noise that seemed to bubble up from beneath his feet, clearly indicating that its origins lay below, perhaps in some large basement area.

Passing numerous doors, Jackson arrived at a doorway, beyond which was the main hall. A wide set of stairs lead up to a wood-panelled landing. Straining his senses, he tried to pinpoint the direction that the sound continued to come from. It seemed closer. His eyes narrowed upon seeing what was obviously supposed to be a concealed door under the stairway lying partially ajar as though the last person who had used it had forgotten to close it. The sound was definitely coming from beyond.

This is where things would get interesting, thought Jackson. There was a tightening in his stomach as he crept closer, his gun now in his hand. There was evil here, of that he was certain. In what manner this evil would manifest itself he didn't know but it was here all the same and with each step he took, that feeling grew stronger.

The malign burbling noise now gave way to a distinctive chant, its tone and words like nothing he had ever heard before.

It was a threatening, soul-rending sound that sent a chill through him and gave him the overall impression that it was not entirely produced by human means. As he paused, listening, he began to hear the low beat of a solitary drum and a shrill piping; a high-pitched whine which cut through his brain like a surgeon's scalpel.

Cautiously, Jackson approached the door. Beyond was a flight of stone steps that led down to a shadowy chamber, the way in which the shadows constantly shifted suggested to him that the area below was lit by flaming torches. There was a faint sooty smell, which reinforced this supposition.

Slowly, he made his way down, certain that any real secrets to be discovered would be found down here. Sure, he could have spent his time going through the dozens of ground and upper floor rooms but it was his intuitive belief that down here was where it was all happening. That there was some kind of ritual ceremony taking place he had little doubt.

Reaching the bottom of the stairs, he moved along a dark, almost tunnel-like stretch of passage at the end of which was an open door. In the poor light, he could see that the walls down here had been painted with Ancient Egyptian hieroglyphics and unsavoury scenes—mostly depicting crocodiles, vultures and giant scorpions devouring people.

Hellish, red light from a hundred torches and candles, emanated from beyond.

The terrible chanting stopped.

Jackson's heart leapt, thinking perhaps that the sudden cessation of sound indicated that he had been spotted. For several unsettling seconds, he just waited, for once genuinely concerned, frightened even. Then the wicked utterances continued, although at a quieter, almost sibilant hiss like that from a nest of aroused cobras. Marshalling his courage, he walked up to the doorway.

The chamber beyond was vast and partly cavernous; some parts of the ceiling supported by pillars, others covered with stalactites. At the far end, fifty yards away, a gathering of figures clad in night-black hooded robes, their backs to him, offered their praises to a large statue of a beast-headed man that stood atop a raised dais. On one side of the infernal idol was a man dressed in full pharaonic regalia; a leopard skin cloak and red robes, complete with a black and red striped *nemes* headdress—a man whom, from the description given by Emerson, was undoubtedly Stourbridge. The latter raised his hands before a stone podium, atop which lay a large tome, and the chanting stopped.

"Brothers in darkness," intoned Stourbridge. "Sons of Set-Peribsen. The time of our Lord's rebirth nears."

The congregation muttered and murmured in shared approval.

"As some of you may know, I will soon be going to our sacred site. There I will receive guidance from our Master—'The Dark Hand of Set.' He informed me recently that the final chambers have been cleared and that we will soon reach the lower levels wherein our ancient brethren are entombed. The deeds that you have all done, the terror and fear that you have all spread, will seem as nothing when our undying brothers are released. Soon this world will know the true meaning of chaos. A new religion will emerge as more and more come to embrace our teachings. For I have gazed into the Black Mirror of Nekhen and looked upon 'The Opener of the Ways.'"

Jackson rubbed his chin. He didn't like much of what he was hearing.

Stourbridge opened the huge book to a specific page. "From the Tenth Chapter of *The Book of Hazareth* as recorded by the Scribe Khyuss. 'And when my king, Set-Peribsen of the Second Dynasty, was cast out of the city, the priests of Nekhen and This brought down a curse upon him, his family, myself and his entire court, dooming all of us to wander nameless and forgotten and to be forever excluded from the Afterlife. Exiled and reviled, we made our way to the Land of Turquoise where as a king, my lord had established mines and forts to strengthen our borders. Here we would exist forever in our undeath, planning and waiting for the aeons to elapse until we would seek our vengeance and once more spread evil and the will of Set, like a pestilence, across the land,'" He looked up. "But know this.

There are those who seek to prevent our holy task. There are those who conspire against us and will do all that they can to thwart our plans. These infidels are to be stopped at all costs. Their eyes are to be gouged from their sockets and thrown to the wild beasts. Their hearts are to be cut from their bodies and trampled into the desert sands where their bones will be gnawed and pecked clean by the hyenas and the carrion birds. One of these, Professor Sidney Emerson, is to be hunted down and slain as soon as possible for it is believed that he possesses a magical ability equivalent to that of our Master."

* * * *

Less than a week later, with the sky a dismal shade of tangerine, Jackson, Emerson and two of the ex-soldier's acquaintances stood on the roof of a small, crude shanty house on the outskirts of Cairo. In every direction, there was a mix of deplorable squalor and poverty, interspersed with towering minarets and the occasional high-rise flat. The Fourth Dynasty pyramids built on the Giza plateau, shrouded in an unsightly cloud of low-lying, industrial smog, dominated the western skyline.

The sunk sank further into the horizon, its descent seeming unnaturally fast. As darkness encroached, a sinister looking half-moon peeped out from the tarnished clouds.

"Murray, are we all ready to head out at first light?" Jackson asked one of his men, a muscled, bearded individual with cropped hair and a crooked nose that had clearly been on the receiving end of too many punches. In his scuffed boots, he stood a good head taller than all of the rest of them.

"Aye. We can go as soon as you like." Murray cracked his knuckles. "We've got two trucks loaded with gear; water, food, weapons. It'll be just like old times. I cannae wait."

"So long as you don't bring along the bagpipes this time," quipped Jackson's man, clicking bullets into his assault rifle. His name was Jennings and he was a crack-shot, supposedly able to shoot the fly off a camel's backside at two hundred yards. "I don't mind getting shot at by murderous Arabs but I'll be damned if I'm going to listen to that bloody racket. No wonder you Jocks drink so much whisky, it's the only way you can put up with the noise."

Murray laughed good-naturedly. "You're probably right, now that I come to think about it."

"Right. Listen up," said Jackson. "We'll go over the plan once more. Tomorrow we travel to Suez and then on to Southern Sinai. Professor, you'll travel with me and Murray. Jennings, you take 'Bully' and Palmer."

"Great." Jennings groaned at the prospect.

'Bully' and Palmer were two of the most obnoxious, crude and belligerent men ever to walk the planet. However, they were also good soldiers and definitely the kind of men one would want on one's side when the going got rough. They were currently off getting some last minute supplies although Jackson had no doubt that they would turn up drunk, having found a bar somewhere or other, Palmer especially, for he had real alcohol problems—indeed, if he wasn't at least half-drunk, it was a problem.

"We'll travel in convoy for safety's sake and rendezvous just outside Abu Zenima before striking out across the desert roads towards Serabit el-Khadim.

"I'm not questioning your authority, 'Wolf,' but do you really think we're going to need as much firepower as you plan on taking?" asked Jennings. "Are we going to start a war or something?"

"Not quite, but you can never be too cautious when out in the badlands as you should know. I've told you all about the Sons of Set-Peribsen. They're well-equipped, well-financed and totally ruthless. Although, that said, I'd be surprised if, when we encounter them, they'll put up much resistance. Still, I'd rather not take any unnecessary risks. We may also have to deal with a bit of weirdness. That's the main reason the professor's here."

"You mentioned this before, but you didn't say much," said Jennings. "What exactly do you mean? Just what is this *weirdness* you're talking about?"

"Aye. It's high time you spilled the beans," agreed Murray. "Just what are we going to be letting ourselves in for? As you know, I don't mind fighting my way out of a crowd of blood-thirsty berserkers intent on cutting me up for mincemeat but I'm not so keen on the idea of dead pharaoh's curses or anything like that."

Jackson didn't know how to respond. He had kept to himself that which he had heard spoken by Stourbridge regarding Emerson having certain powers—not having even told the professor himself, although he felt, deep down, that perhaps that had been a mistake. However, he had made mention that some high-up in the cult, a certain Ibrahim Bashakti, also known as 'The Dark Hand of Set' may have sorcerous powers and that great care should be taken if encountered. The normal members of the Brotherhood were, as far as he was aware, just misguided men; indoctrinated, radicalised slaves to a malevolent and heretical orthodoxy.

"I can assure you that there won't be any mumbo-jumbo." It was Emerson who answered the Scotsman's question. "There are no such things as dark powers in this day and age. That these men who may be out there are evil, I have no doubt, but that's all they are. Evil men." Despite all he had been through and all he had subsequently discovered whether through personal experience or through research, the professor still held to the view that this was surely a task best suited for the local authorities. It was the lure of finding and exploring these unknown rock-cut tombs that forced him to go along with this. There was also the possibility of finding some clues as to the tragic fate of his expedition members. Additionally, whatever else he thought of Jackson, the man had saved his life.

"You have heard it from the professor. There's nothing to worry about. Right, I don't know about you lot but I'm going to turn in for the night. We have got quite a busy day ahead of us tomorrow." Jackson turned and headed downstairs.

* * * *

The going became harder as the desert road they had been following became little more than a meandering trail through the rocky wilderness. The area was inhospitable, the late afternoon sun, cruel and unforgiving in its fierce intensity. Huge clouds of dust and sand, thrown up by the truck in front added to the difficult and dangerous driving conditions. There were no longer any signposts giving directions. This truly was a land forgotten; a dead, broken land of red rock, sand and long-dried up river beds—wadis, which in ancient times had been important trade routes and 'roads' allowing access to rich raw materials; copper, turquoise, malachite, sandstone and basalt.

"How are you enjoying it so far, professor?" asked Jackson, shifting gear so that he could pick up speed in order to keep up with the vehicle ahead.

"I'm not." The constant bumping, the wind-blown grit and the malodorous stale body odour coming from Murray whom Emerson was sat beside all contributed to making it a very unpleasant journey. In addition, he had reason to dislike this place for this is where he had lost ten members of his research team under circumstances still unexplained. It was also where he himself had come close to death. His inability to remember those last days worried him and the occasional flash of strange images that he had begun to have were unsettling. The previous night he had dreamed of huge wings before waking in a sweat. Checking the few landmarks, he called to Jackson. "We can't be that far from Serabit el-Khadim now, can we?"

"About another five miles. However, we'll be taking a southern trail before we get there. We continue along that for another fifteen miles or so." Steering wheel in one hand, Jackson took a swig from his water canteen.

The remainder of the journey went past in an uncomfortable blur of billowing dust and blistering heat. The scenery remained largely uniform, for there was no vegetation out here, no buildings or landmarks, no people—at least no visible ones, although Jackson clung to the suspicion that their progress was being tracked. Consequently, he was forever checking his mirrors and scanning the rugged horizons for any tell-tale flashes, reflections which would reveal the presence of others.

The lead truck slowed down and then came to a stop.

"Is this the place?" asked Emerson, looking around.

"Yes. Here we are." Jackson pulled up next to the other truck and switched off the engine. Opening the door, he jumped down and went over to have a word with Jennings who had now exited his vehicle. He came stomping back shortly after, his face tight and stern. "Jennings was telling me that he thinks he saw movement up on that ridge over there." He pointed to the place in question. "I don't like the fact that we're sitting ducks at the moment so we're going to venture a bit further as I know a more defensible and secure place. Once there, we'll set up base." He gave a quick glance around before getting back in the truck and starting it up again.

Ten minutes later both trucks pulled into a narrow-mouthed canyon with suitable exit points to the north and east. The rocky cliff-faces were relatively low and yet devoid of hiding places where snipers could hide in wait. It was hidden and secret, or so Jackson thought, and less than twenty minutes by foot from where the rock-cut tombs were located.

Once they had parked up and 'Bully' and Murray had assumed their defensive positions, the remainder of the group set about putting up tents and awnings, efficiently going about their business of making an ideal campsite all under the gaze of Emerson. Three tents, made from camouflaged material were quickly erected, as was a small cooking area. Palmer soon had a fire going and steaming coffee was being distributed in metal tankards.

"We'll stay here an hour or so. We'll then go and see what exactly is happening at the place marked 'X.'" Jackson poured a tot of whisky into his coffee mug and took a drink.

"Have you any ideas as to what could be happening?" asked Emerson.

"Whatever it is, it can't be good." Jackson took a combat knife from his belt and began picking his fingernails with it. "Truth be told, I don't know what we're going to face when we get there. Could be that they're empty, but if what I heard at that meeting back in England's anything to go by I think there could be some real trouble. And I'm not just talking of the flying bullets variety either."

"You still think there's something strange going on, don't you?"

Jackson exhaled a lungful of breath. It felt as though he was expunging his lungs of a thousand years of deposited sand. There was a fiery burn in his throat. "I don't know what to think. I guess we'll have to wait and see. What I will say is, be ready for anything."

"What exactly are you expecting? Do you honestly think there will be a shootout?"

"That's hard to say. I sincerely hope not, but my men have very itchy trigger fingers and I for one, wouldn't want to be in the sandals of any of these cult members if they try anything. I don't suppose you've seen Palmer's modified, tripod-mounted, Vickers machine gun, have you? On top of that, you'll be pleased to know that Murray's got enough dynamite in the truck to blow Mount Sinai to pieces. Last time you came here you only had trowels and brushes. This time, however, you're with people armed to the teeth. People who know how to fight back." Jackson fastened a hand-grenade to his belt.

* * * *

Night had fallen. The sky was a brilliant tapestry of stars, and the bright, lurid moonlight washed over everything, creating an alien, lunar landscape filled with shadows. It was now mercifully cool with only a residual heat from the day remaining and the air was still, enabling the slightest sound to carry for miles. And there were sounds; the slither and fall of loose rubble from a scree slope or the distant, haunting call of a lone jackal or bird of prey.

Outfitted in his desert camouflage gear, like that of his men, his face smeared with lampblack, Jackson raised his hand, signalling to those following him to stop. He then edged forward. Peering from behind a large boulder, he could see the shadowy, rectangular-shaped tomb mouths that riddled the cliff face some fifty yards away. From where he crouched, he could tell that there had been quite intensive work carried out at the site for several of the openings had been shored-up with wooden scaffolding and there were barrels, boxes and numerous wheelbarrows stacked rather haphazardly at some of the entrances. Some of the higher tombs were accessed only by rickety ladders.

Parked at the base of the cliff there were three large trucks not dissimilar to the ones they had, as well as two dust-covered cars and a motorbike.

He could see no one around although dim light came from one of the nearest openings.

"Looks like they've been carrying out their own little excavations," said Emerson, taking in the scene before him. "I wonder just what they think they're going to unearth?"

Jackson slammed a clip into his submachine gun. "I say we go and find out." With a circling hand motion, he silently instructed his men to start filling out, to keep down and advance towards the steep incline which gave access to the lowest of the rock cut-tombs, the one from which the light emanated.

That these tombs were ancient and quite conceivably Early Dynastic in origin, Emerson now no longer doubted. They were strange and certainly atypical, unusual in the sense that they were so unlike the *mastaba* brick-built elite tombs at Abydos and Saqqara or even the more commonplace covered pits reserved for the lower echelons of Ancient Egyptian society. He found himself pausing for a minute, realizing the significance of this archaeological find, his academic thoughts temporarily coming to the surface regardless of the dangers of the current situation.

Jennings gave him a tap on the shoulder. "Professor. We should be moving."

"Quiet back there," hissed Jackson. Submachine gun in hand, he crept forward. Using the cliff wall for cover, he glanced inside the tunnel entrance. Noting nothing untoward, he signalled for Murray and 'Bully' to join him. Shadows seemed to lurk unnaturally at the inner walls of the hewn surfaces and, even at the entrance, the air was stale and stifling. Powdered rock drizzled from the ceiling and, despite recent attempts to shore up the walls the place looked incredibly unsafe as though, despite the fact that it had endured close on five thousand years, it could collapse at any moment.

Slowly and stealthily, the men made their way deeper into the passage. On either side dark openings led to narrower passages, the stench coming from them terribly foul, as of things long-buried. It appeared that the cliff was honeycombed with such tunnels and that they were now worming their way deeper towards the centre like maggots burrowing their way to the core of an apple. From somewhere up ahead they could hear the sound of a deep male voice chanting words that no human tongue had made for close on five millennia. They had to be nearing the inner sanctum.

The sight that loomed before Jackson and his men was like something from the pits of Hell for the cavernous chamber they now overlooked was aglow with numerous flaming torches set in conveniently positioned brackets secured to the walls. It was a massive area hollowed inside the cliff and it had been transformed into a place of worship for The Sons of Set-Peribsen. To this end, a huge central dais had been installed around which some two dozen dark hooded figures had gathered, forming a circle. In the centre, standing by a large statue of their infernal god was Stourbridge, dressed once more in his pharaonic regalia. A large Arab, similarly dressed, stood beside him. He held aloft a long cobra-headed staff and it was he who was calling out the strange words.

At the back of the cavern was a huge pit from which wreathes of dense violet smoke spiralled and steamed like viperous wraiths. Chains slithered down into its Stygian depths.

"That man next to Stourbridge. That must be Bashakti. 'The Dark Hand of Set,'" whispered Jackson.

"Do you have a plan?" asked Emerson.

Jackson grinned. "No. Have you?" He was about to say something else when the chanting stopped. There then came a shrill scream and from an opening over to his right a scrawny line of shackled prisoners were led out by two of the dark-robed worshippers.

"Good Lord! They're still alive!" said Emerson.

"Your expedition members, I take it?"

"Yes. But—"

The column of human misery was being taken towards the pit and it seemed pretty obvious that they were going to be sacrificed.

"Okay, let's move it." Jackson and his men scrambled down from where they were hidden.

Bashakti and Stourbridge stared at them. For a moment it was they who didn't know how to react, believing that their inner temple was well hidden from prying eyes and that no one in their right minds would dare challenge them, at least not here of all places.

The Dark Brotherhood turned and that was when true chaos erupted. For these were not the human followers of the cult Jackson had seen back in England. These were the true Sons of Set-Peribsen; shrivelled, desiccated, withered mummies in dark robes, their stinking remains cursed with undeath. Eternally damned; their souls forever unable to enter the Afterlife these were the original followers of Set-Peribsen. Howling their wrath, they came at Jackson and his men, khopeshes—vicious, curved, scimitar-like swords—and daggers grasped in their rotted, partially skeletal hands. Some were partially bound in stained linen bandages into which had been incorporated ancient trinkets, scarabs and tarnished items of copper jewellery. An intense hatred of all that did not worship Set burned in the lambent red glow within their eye-sockets.

Despite all of the dangers he had faced, Jackson's nerve faltered. Never in his life had he experienced fear of this magnitude. Whether it was due to his intense hatred of the cult or for some other reason, from somewhere he got the mental reserve to stand his ground. Levelling his submachine gun at the approaching horde, he opened fire, a stream of bullets blasting through the cloaked zombies.

More gunfire echoed around the chamber, the air now filled with the scent of cordite as Jackson's men gunned down more and more of the mummies. Screams and shouts reverberated off the walls. The prisoners were yelling, desperately crying out to be rescued.

A grenade exploded, sending tattered remains, bones and weapons into the air.

A shrivelled head rolled to Jackson's feet and with horror he saw that it was still moving, the mouth and grotesquely decayed teeth snapping to bite him. He gave it a powerful kick before raining a second burst of submachine gunfire into the foul horde.

"They're not dying!" shouted Murray. With a curse, he blasted a mummy at close range with his shotgun, blowing its head from its scrawny shoulders. The thing staggered to its feet before drunkenly righting itself whereupon he shot it a second time, knocking it back into the path of two more.

Suddenly 'Bully' and Jennings were screaming as more of the undead rushed from a tunnel opening, cutting the two of them off from the others. Trapped and outnumbered, the two men stood back-to-back and cut down swathes of the creatures before being overrun by the ghastly Sons of Set-Peribsen. In one terrible instant, Jackson saw Jennings being dragged to the ground and bloodily hacked to death.

Matters were made worse when Bashakti raised his staff and brought down a pillar of raging fire on Murray. Wreathed in a whirling vortex of flame, the tall, bearded Scotsman staggered through the mass of grasping zombies, setting some of them alight before making a desperate lunge at Stourbridge. Grasping him in a tight embrace, he made a mad dive for the open pit and the two of them disappeared over the edge.

Of all Jackson's men it was Palmer the alcoholic who ended up the main hero of the day. For while the battle had been raging he had been freeing the line of prisoners, marshalling them and getting them out. Most of them were only too willing to be liberated and given the chance of escape but some were scared and need coaxing. Having now secured the release of all ten of them and, realizing that they were now pitted against a foe that they could not defeat, he deemed it high time to escape. Providing a burst of covering fire for Jackson, he screamed at Emerson to get out.

Although most of the mummies had been blown to pieces, whether from bullets or from flying shrapnel, they were still animate; dismembered heads and limbs rolling and crawling, seeking to rejoin with their parent bodies.

Jackson saw Bashakti raise his staff and ran for the exit, a sheet of fire engulfing the area where he had just been standing. He felt the heat as flames licked out and burnt his back. His hair was singed.

There was mad, blind panic now as the recently liberated prisoners, Emerson, Palmer and Jackson ran along the tunnel. From behind them came the cries and the howls of the damned. Jackson turned and sprayed a hail of bullets before his clip emptied, the flash of gunfire illuminating the headless and limbless horrors that poured out of the darkness. Unclipping a hand grenade from his belt, he tossed it into the gathering and sprinted for the exit.

There followed a muffled explosion and the passage was filled almost instantly with thick black smoke. The walls trembled and one of the recently fitted support beams cracked and buckled. A gaping fissure opened along one wall.

Then they were out, scampering down the slope, heading for the parked vehicles.

"Everybody into the trucks!" Jackson shouted. He turned to Palmer. "Have you got any grenades left?"

"I'm all out."

"Damn!" Jackson had planned to collapse the tomb opening, hoping against hope that it was the only point of egress from the inner sanctum, thus entombing Bashakti and the Dark Brotherhood. Luck was once again shining on him for suddenly the tomb mouth did collapse, the damage wrought by his earlier explosion causing the age-old tunnel ceiling to give way. With an almighty crash, the rock-cut tomb mouth came down, sending forth a great billowing cloud of sand and dust.

Jackson and Palmer cheered, their cries of jubilation added to by some of the members of Emerson's expedition.

But then, out from the destruction stepped Bashakti. He appeared unharmed, unscathed. "You think that I'll let you get away? You think that I can be defeated so easily?" Grasping at his forehead, he ripped away a strip of flesh from his face. An unsightly, ragged flap of skin hung loose. He pulled harder and it came free as though it were a gruesome Halloween mask—only in this case the monster lurked beneath it—revealing a yellowy-brown skull. Howling his anger, he began to shake, the skin in which he had encased himself splitting and crumbling, falling free and piling as dust around his feet. Soon all that remained was a leathery, skeletal, shrunken corpse. "*I am Set-Peribsen!* I was old when the pyramids were still stone in their quarries and the Sphinx had yet to rise from the sands. I call upon Set, the Supreme Lord of Desolation, to destroy you all." The undead pharaoh threw down his staff and raised his withered arms.

With a violent tremor, the ground shook. Thunder and lightning filled the air and despite the desert atmosphere a rain of hailstones started to fall, bombarding them.

Stunned, horrified, Jackson stumbled to one knee. A crack in the earth opened up nearby and the hailstones were now striking like sling stones. Getting to his feet he ran for cover, leaping into one of the trucks at which one of the expedition members was behind the wheel. Fortunately the ignition keys were still there and the man started the engine and threw the gears into reverse, pulling the vehicle back as another crack appeared in the ground. For one terrible moment one of the front tyres was caught. Smoking, it whined and turned before finding purchase enabling the truck to move.

"Right, let's get the hell out of—" Jackson stopped and stared, open-mouthed. A huge ring of fire erupted from the ground, encompassing them, sealing off all means of escape. They were trapped and now at the mercy of the merciless. Such was the ferocity of the heat, he knew they wouldn't be able to drive through it without being cremated, not even at speed. Through the hail, the fire and the chaos, illuminated in the headlights of the truck, he saw Emerson, whom he thought was in the other truck with Palmer. The elderly Egyptologist stood facing the nightmare that was Set-Peribsen.

What happened next shook even Jackson's war-hardened sanity. It was a sorcerous battle, a conflict that breached the bounds of madness and threatened to tip him into the abyss of inescapable insanity. One moment he saw a mass of striking cobras and stinging scorpions manifest in the air around Emerson only to be consumed in a blast of blue fire that shot from the professor's fingers. Then there was a cloud of darkness that lasted for a minute or so before being dispelled and Set-Peribsen was sent spinning, green electric-like sparks covering the cursed pharaoh from head to foot. Emerson himself looked unnaturally calm, his eyes closed as his hands moved in patterns through the air.

Still the hail was striking, thumping constantly off the truck.

Jackson shook away his fleeting sense of unreality and focused his eyes, trying to take in exactly what was happening.

With a bloodcurdling scream and a dark flash, Set-Peribsen once more tore free from his current form. A ravenous, long-snouted composite beast, part jackal, part man, snarled and spat. Clawed hands grasped Emerson. The thing's jaw widened and it took a chunk out of the professor's throat before dashing him to the rocky ground. It stood over his corpse, gloatingly. Jackson let out a choked cry at the sight of the crumpled body.

Suddenly a dark shadow fell about Set-Peribsen.

With a high-pitched screech a gigantic, fiery hawk sped down, grasped the monstrous thing in its outstretched talons and carried it up. The hawk turned, high in the air, then went into a dive. As it hurtled towards the ground, the fiery corona around it increased and the bird and the undead pharaoh hit the ground in an almighty explosion.

The ring of fire disappeared. The hailstones and the seismic convulsions stopped.

"Did you see that?" The young man next to Jackson stared wide-eyed. "That hawk. It's just like the professor told me."

"What do you mean?"

"The hawk of Horus. It was Horus who defeated Set. Professor Emerson once told me that when he worked out in Nekhen an old Egyptian had told him that he believed him to be a reincarnation of one of the high priests of the Hawk-god. Of course he had disbelieved it, but it's true. When our camp-site was raided, I didn't see the professor in the confusion but I heard a hawk crying overhead."

"What else can you tell me?"

"Only that Doctor Stourbridge had us work in the tombs. We had no means of escape and they forced us to dig until only a day or so ago we found the actual burial of Set-Peribsen. Scholars had long thought that Petrie excavated his tomb at Abydos but obviously not. When Bashakti arrived the dead pharaoh took possession of his body." He shuddered. "I hope never to see such a thing again."

Jackson and Palmer passed out water canteens among the rescued men then went to examine the mortal remains of Professor Emerson. The bloody tear in his throat was at odds with the serene expression on his face and the impression on the sand around him of immense wings.

THE HORROR AT
THURLBURY MANOR

*Sometimes the darkest deeds are
done in the sleepiest of places....*

The village of Thurlbury was set in the pleasant countryside of south-east England. It was a peaceful, bucolic backwater that prided itself on having one of the best cricket teams in the area. Nothing unforeseen happened in the village, the regular rhythm of its rural life continued from year to year with only minor changes. The horse-drawn vehicle had gradually given ways to cars but the progress of the big cities had yet to challenge Thurlbury's complacency.

Even so, inside the small Thurlbury police station things were getting quite heated. For the second time that week, Eric Wheeler, the oldest man in the village and by far the most cantankerous was venting his spleen.

"If I was ten years younger I'd have caught the little blighters," he wheezed.

Sergeant Doug Russell doubted that very much. Thirty years, maybe, he thought to himself. "Well, as I said Mr. Wheeler, I'll be sure to go and have a word with their parents. Now, if there's—"

"You make bloody sure that you do." Eric's face was drawn tight. "I'm not havin' those ragamuffins sneakin' into my orchard an' pinchin' my apples. That's both trespassin' an' theft. An' I don't care if they're nine-year-olds or ninety-year-olds, it's my property." His face was flushed as red as a beetroot, his knobbly fingers clenched tight around his walking stick. "A damn good hidin' is what they're needin'."

Arthritically, he got to his feet.

With a surreptitious glance at his wristwatch, Russell was somewhat relieved to see it was fast approaching six o'clock. It would soon be time for him to lock up and leave—as soon as he got rid of this geriatric nuisance. Kids would be kids, he told himself, thinking back to the numerous instances when, as a boy, he had indulged in a little bit of apple scrumping. Yes, technically, it could be considered illegal, but it was a crime that he was well prepared to turn a blind eye to. In the main reception room he could hear the phone ringing. It was answered by his constable, a young man named Walters.

"I'm tellin' you, sergeant, if I catch them at it again. Why, I'll…" With a disgruntled shake of his fist the old man turned his back on Russell and made for the door. He stood there for a moment and then returned to the desk. "If Sergeant Willis were still here he'd have sorted them out. He didn't stand for any of this."

"Sergeant Willis has retired, I'm afraid to say. But rest assured, Mr. Wheeler, I will endeavour to restore law and order to Thurlbury by apprehending these two young villains of the peace."

"I hope you're not makin' a fool of me or the seriousness of this crime. Back in the old days they'd have had their hands—"

"Sergeant!" Walters stood in the doorway. From the look on his face and the urgency in his voice it was clear to Russell that something far more serious than the theft of several apples from Eric Wheeler's orchard had transpired. The constable looked at Eric, wondering whether to relate his news in the presence of the other.

"Well…what is it?" asked Russell.

"That was Father Barton on the phone. He was calling from the phone box just outside St. Leonard's. He said that he's found a body. A dead person."

"Are you sure?" Russell could feel a tingling in his nerves. "Did he tell you anything else? Any details?"

"Er, yes. Although I'm not sure how believable they are. He said that the body seemed to be…well…wrapped up in something."

"Wrapped up? Like a Christmas present?" quipped Eric.

Russell threw a disapproving glance at the old man, clearly finding nothing amusing in his unwelcome and disrespectful comment.

"No. He said it was more like spider webs."

* * * *

Less than ten minutes later Russell and Walters arrived at St. Leonard's. It was a bright summer's evening and parking up and getting out of the car the two policemen were met at the old lych-gate by the village priest. One glance was enough to detect the shock imprinted on his ashen face.

"I'm so relieved you've come. It's horrible," Barton blurted out. "I've never seen anything like it. I saw him come stumbling into the graveyard. He was covered in white dust. At first I thought it was talcum powder. Then I thought it was asbestos. After he'd fallen, the webs grew over him."

"Steady now, Father," said Russell. "Why don't you show me where the body is."

Barton led them past the edge of the church towards the far side of the graveyard. "It's almost as though he's been wound up in a giant spider web or something. It must be the work of the Devil."

Upon reaching the grisly web-bound remains the two policeman let out faint exclamations of shock and revulsion—more so at the smell that was coming from it than at the actual sight.

"Bloody hell," muttered Russell. He stood looking down, hands on hips. If it were not for the dusty shoes, which protruded from the mass of grey-white bindings he would have figured it impossible that a human being could have been encased within. Looking around him, surveying the scene, he noticed tatters of similar stuff snared to the hawthorn bushes over to his right.

"Do you think he was trying to get inside the church?" suggested Barton.

"Quite possibly." Russell stared down at the body.

"Do you think he might be that bloke who was reported wandering along the road between here and Crowhaven earlier this evening?" asked Walters.

"He might be." Russell removed a thick pair of leather gloves from his coat pocket and put them on. "Let's just see what we've got here shall we?"

"You aren't going to touch that stuff are you?" asked Barton concernedly. "When I first saw the body I'm sure there were things moving within it. Spiders, probably."

"I'll be all right with my gloves on. After all, I don't see any signs of movement now and I don't think this stuff's acidic."

"What if it's some kind of weird disease?" ventured Walters. "You know, something from Outer Space. I've seen things like this at the cinema. *Invasion of the Body Snatchers*. He'll turn into—"

"Just shut up, will you? Besides, who's in charge here?" Cautiously, the sergeant rubbed at a portion of the strange material that was surprisingly not as tough or as coarse as he, or the other two had expected. It proved to be somewhat sticky, possessing adhesive properties as evidenced by the manner in which swathes of it were gluing to his gloves. "It's like candyfloss," he observed curiously, wiping several layers away as he sought to get to the body within, a look of growing revulsion on his face. The more he cleared, the worse the smell got and at such proximity to it, he felt like vomiting. Somehow, he maintained his composure and continued with his unsavoury task, deeming it vitally important to at least try and see if he could obtain any means of identifying the victim—assuming, that was, that the unfortunate was dead. For there was a slim chance that whoever it was could still be alive. After all, he had once read in some natural history magazine that certain spiders kept their prey paralysed in their webs, storing them for later, preferring their snacks alive.

"I can see feet, but are you *sure* there's a man in there?" asked Walters.

"Well, there's something...nearly, there..." Russell was now delving deeply into the husk-like remnants. Pulling clear the final strands from the cocoon, he found himself gazing down into the sickly pale face of Bradley Higgins—a man whose photograph featured predominantly on several of the notice boards and in his ledger of wanted rogues back at the police station. Admittedly, the face in the photographs lacked the chalk-white, seemingly lifeless, features, but it was Higgins all the same. "Well, well."

"Do you know him?" ventured Barton after the initial shock at seeing the grisly spectacle had subsided.

"Indeed I do. Bradley Higgins." The sergeant rose to his feet. "A petty thief. Wanted on several counts of burglary. God knows what's happened to him though. I can't for the life of me think of anything that could've caused this."

A few seconds of muted silence followed as each of the three men gazed down in numbed perplexity.

It was Walters who broke the silence. "What about that supposedly top-secret army base over in Wrexley? You know, that place where they experiment on all sorts of things. I had a cousin who worked there five years ago and some of the things he told me—"

"Wrexley's been closed down for the past two years," interrupted Russell.

"Yeah, sure. Do you believe that? Places like that are never closed down. We're just told that so they can continue with their work away from scrutiny. Heard tell that shortly after the war they were using that place as a base for research into biological and chemical weapons. Nerve gas and highly contagious and lethal diseases. All that kind of nice stuff. I used to see army trucks going up to the gates at all hours of the day. Strange thing how I never saw any coming out."

"Well, be that as it may, what are we going to do with him?" asked Barton. "After all, he can't stay here...although he'll probably end up here, if you know what I mean," the priest added as an afterthought.

"You're right, Father." Russell turned to his constable. "Go back to the car and radio for an ambulance, will you? Tell them that we've got a body at St. Leonard's. Tell them—" He broke off wondering just what exactly his constable should tell them. It was then that he saw a green car pull up beside the parked police vehicle. A short, suited man got out and hurriedly made his way over to them. "Christ, this is all we need," he cursed upon noticing who it was. It was Arthur Bowden, the village school headmaster.

"Sergeant Russell." Bowden jogged the remaining distance that separated them, his fleshy face reddening with the exertion. "I thought I'd just inform you that there's something very peculiar happening over at the Manor house. I was—" He stopped, mid-sentence, his jaw dropping open, noticing for the first time the gruesome package on the ground. And then the smell hit him.

"Good God! What on earth?!"

"A most unfortunate and as yet unexplained tragedy," said Russell. "Worry not, however, for things are now under control. So if you'd just tell me—"

"The Manor? Yes, of course," Bowden had trouble taking his eyes from the horrible thing on the ground such was his macabre fascination with it. After all, a man encased in weird webbing, his features seemingly drained of blood, was not something one saw every day.

"Well…?"

"Well…I think the two must be related. I was driving home when I heard what sounded like a muffled explosion. At first I thought it might have been something to do with the army base at Wrexley but then I saw a plume of dirty white smoke drifting over the trees in the opposite direction to the Wrexley Road. Naturally, I thought that there had been an accident somewhere so I headed towards where it had come from and when I got to the old Manor gates, I saw a cloud of grey smoke hanging over the west wing of the building. The gates were closed so I could go no further. However I did see that there were several cars parked in the grounds."

"I was under the impression that the Manor house was untenanted," said Barton.

"It is as far as I know," added Russell. He quickly mentally added two and two. "Unless of course Higgins and some of his gang were carrying out a little raid there. Yes, it's all becoming clearer."

"Is it?" His constable looked doubtful.

"In what way?" added Barton.

Russell hesitated, it *was* hard to see how the two events could be linked. For while it was feasible that Higgins had staggered across country and along the winding rural lanes the three miles or so that separated St. Leonard's from the Manor house there was surely nothing within that old ruin which could have caused this. He was a man who always sought the easiest explanation even if, in a case such as this, there was no clear explanation. Nevertheless the picture that was forming in his head was one of a botched robbery. Either there had been an accident or Higgins' accomplices had done this to one of their own and right now, if the headmaster's account could be believed, the possibility was that the rest of the gang were up there at the Manor or had been not that long ago. Perhaps there had been an explosion—an underground mine or something. It could be that the thieves had discovered some underground tunnels built beneath the Manor and had unwittingly stumbled upon a pocket of explosive gas; old vents brimming with methane and some weird subterranean mineral which hardened and crystallised over time before reverting back to a sticky substance. Stranger things had happened, he tried to tell himself. His meandering attempts to find an explanation were not working, he needed more to go on. He pulled himself together. "Well, if Higgins is related to events up at the Manor then I think it's vitally important that I get up there and see what's going on. Particularly if that's the site of this explosion you heard."

"Without doubt." Bowden nodded. "And as I said, there was a murky grey cloud hanging over the place." He turned his gaze in that direction but due to the lie of the land and the woods in the vicinity nothing untoward was visible. "If it wasn't for the trees, I'm sure you'd be able to see it."

"Right. Father, I'd appreciate it if you stayed here with Mr. Bowden whilst we go and discover what's happening up at the Manor. I'll put a call through for an ambulance to pick up Mr. Higgins." He looked at Bowden, well aware that he was one of the worst gossips in the village. "For the time being I'd like this kept between us until we know what we're dealing with. I don't want you going around causing panic. Understand?" Privately he doubted whether the other would pay a blind bit of notice to his caution. He would go straight to *The Plough*, the sole public house in Thurlbury whereupon no doubt, virtually everyone in the village would know within an hour or two.

* * * *

Russell stood by the parked police car cursing his ill-fortune. For, less than five minutes drive from St. Leonard's, the car had had a puncture, prompting them to stop and make a change of tyre. Despite Walter's relatively good grasp of basic car maintenance it had still taken the best part of a quarter of an hour and he was acutely aware of how much time was of the essence.

Consequently, there was a growing knot of apprehension in the sergeant's stomach that he was finding hard to shift as he sat in the passenger seat of the police car when they eventually approached Thurlbury Manor, a building that had been built in the mid-seventeenth century. He could see the cloud of smoke the headmaster had mentioned, its vapours now drifting on the wind, carrying with it the malodorous reek that was now proving worryingly familiar.

"What's your take on this, sir?" asked Walters, changing gear as they now neared the tall wrought-iron gates, beyond which stretched a length of private drive leading to the Manor itself. Through the bars they could see several cars parked within.

"To tell you the truth, I'm not sure." It was an honest enough response.

At the gate they parked and got out.

"That smell's horrible. There's a chemical tang to it. I hope to God it's not toxic."

Russell turned to his constable and nodded in agreement. There was no denying the fact that the stench was truly horrendous. Walking up to the gates he gave one a sharp tug, unsurprised to find it was securely locked by a thick length of chain at the end of which was secured a stout padlock.

"I'll get the crowbar," commented Walters. "Probably best if we can get this gate open."

For a moment the sergeant ignored the recommendation. There was something not quite right going on, something which rattled his nerves. For the briefest of moments he tried to rationalise just what that was. Then it struck him—surely it stood to reason that if some calamity or other had befallen those inside the house then some of them at least would have made good their escape and taken their cars. Where were the survivors gathered around outside? Surely whatever had occurred had not been as utterly calamitous as to kill them all—leaving Higgins the sole escapee? If that were the case then it was clear that this tragedy was of tremendous proportions. It was as he was thinking through the various scenarios that presented themselves to his troubled mind that he witnessed his constable pry the chain loose with the aid of the crowbar he had got from the boot of the car. With a push, the gate swung open, grating protestingly on un-oiled hinges.

There was a detectable awfulness in the air that was almost tangible; a foulness that was not of this Earth and one that was not solely due to the horrendous odour that pervaded everything. If one imagined hard enough it was even tasteable; a slimy vileness that brought instant nausea to the stomach and weakness to the limbs. If evil was ever bottled and sold to the malign there was no doubt this was how it would taste.

A sudden chill descended, enshrouding the two policemen as they stared uncertainly at the mystifying spectacle before them. For the once-grand Manor house, which had fallen into disrepair and neglect having been untenanted for many years, had been transformed into something from a nightmarish fairytale.

In the fading light, they could see that much of it was covered in that peculiar grey-white dust from which grotesque, web-like strands sprouted, festooning huge swathes of the ancient architecture. From the looks of it most of it had erupted from smashed windows, the wide-open front door and the chimney stacks, supporting the supposition that something within had exploded, blasting the foul-looking soot-like substance out.

"What the hell?" exclaimed Walters, eyes-wide in stunned disbelief.

Commonsense was shrieking at Russell to get as far from this detestable place as was possible, to get back in the police car and put a good number of miles between them and Thurl-bury Manor. Yet something else prompted him to investigate further. With a nervous gulp, he started forward. For a brief moment fear threatened to hold him rigid, although he managed to overcome it, intrigued now as to just what had happened here. Mentally, he wrestled with the very unreality of it all, trying to assimilate the facts and bring order to what lay before him. Upon seeing something like this he was almost prepared to accept his constable's earlier theory of alien intervention, after all this surely defied all known terrestrial explanations.

"Look at this, sir," said Walters, pointing to the gravel drive. "Footprints."

Russell looked to where Walters indicated, thankful at least to divert his vision from the sickening contagion that clung, like an unearthly parasite, to the Manor. There were indeed foot-prints, easily discernible due to their white, chalk-like outlines. They left a trail that led from the front door, across the wide lawn, along a portion of the drive before petering out in the direction of the perimeter wall where a rope dangled from an overhanging branch.

"So that explains how Higgins got out."

"Do you think it's a good idea to go in there?" Walters asked nervously. "I mean maybe we should see about calling for back-up from Melbury and Chaddinham. There's six cars here so that means there could be—"

"Come on, show a bit of backbone, will you?" There was touch of bravado in Russell's voice but that's all it really was. In reality he was feeling just as apprehensive—and dare he admit, frightened—as his colleague. Nevertheless, he knew it was his duty to find out what was going on and there was also the like-lihood that there were injured people inside. Any delay could prove fatal.

"Well, after you." There was a mirthless grin on Walter's face as he stared into the shadowy mouth of the front doorway. Unclipping a small torch that hung at his belt he handed it over. "Just in case this explosion has shorted the electrics."

Russell switched on the torch. One glance was sufficient for him to recognise the main hallway although this room was now in a severe state of neglect and decay. Dust and cobwebs were everywhere, festooning the antique Victorian furniture, clog-ging the corners with sticky strands and dangling like ghostly hair from a central chandelier. Mildewed wallpaper hung in long strips from the walls. Upon entering, something brushed against his face and he knocked it away with his hands, his head jerk-ing involuntarily back. The scuff of their shoes seemed oddly amplified as they edged forward.

The footprints they had followed from outside left a clear trail in the dust, heading for the far corridor that led into the rear of the building. In places could be seen the occasional splotch of dusted-over blood.

"This place is giving me the creeps," commented Walters, his eyes darting all around.

Russell nodded. With delicate steps, avoiding the footprints, he edged his way forward, the light from the torch throwing weird shadows before him. Was it just his overwrought imagina-tion or were there small dark shapes scuttling within the denser patches of web? Shining the torchlight up the stairs he saw a huge swathe of web spanning from floor to ceiling.

The dust underfoot crunched like powdered snow—al-though the impression Russell had was of stepping on a thick layer of dead cockroaches. It grew noticeably darker the further they went from the main door; the dim light which now shone through the obscured windows offering little illumination. In addition to the footprints and the drops of blood there could also be seen marks on the walls indicative of places where someone—presumably Higgins—had dragged a hand along the surface.

Before them, the corridor made a sharp right turn.

Russell looked at his constable who gave an emphatic shake of his head, demonstrating his heartfelt reluctance to go any further. With a grim smile, he steeled himself and crept forward, sneaking up to the corner whereupon he peeked out. Raising his torch, he shone the beam straight in front of him, aware that his hand was trembling.

Shadows danced and shifted as he directed the torchlight into the chamber that lay at the end of the short stretch of dust-covered corridor. Whether the large room had once served as a dining hall or a spacious reception area it was hard to tell for it had been cleared of all furniture. Thick drapes had been pulled across all of the windows and there were no other visible exits.

In the middle of the room, sat or crouched on the floor were nine shapes, arms outstretched, hands clasped, forming a ring. In the centre of this ghastly circle was a grotesque lump some twelve feet high; a hideous grey-green growth which sprouted up from the ground like a bizarre toadstool, its top almost touching the ceiling. Obscene secretions oozed from unsightly pores, trickling down its ugly surfaces and pooling around it. It seemed abundantly clear to Russell that this was the 'epicentre' for this weird happening.

"What the hell?" Walters had found the courage to come up and was now staring about him in morbid curiosity.

"Jesus!" Cautiously, Russell entered the room, his torch held out before him like an amulet to ward off evil. Panning the light over several of the linked figures, he could see that they all appeared very dead; their faces and hands withered, almost mummified. Under the dust and the webbing that covered some of them could be seen strange black robes bearing odd cabbalistic designs. One of the nine was hooded and wore a bizarre symbol around his neck.

"God Almighty!" exclaimed Walters. "Devil worshippers! Here—in Thurlbury!"

Insanity threatened to scream at him and for a moment Russell was at a loss for words. He wandered around the circle like a man in a nightmare panning his torch over the cadaverous, age-worn features. He had the terrible feeling that they were watching him, following his every movement; that he was being tracked by the sightless eyes of these dead men. He could feel the fear flooding over his body like a river of sheer evil, touching him with an icy heat that bit into his limbs so that every nerve screamed in protest. Desperately, he forced himself to shrug it away and continued with his inspection although any identification was impossible such was the advanced state of decay. There was obviously a clear link between what had happened here and what had befallen Higgins.

"And what's that thing in the middle?"

Russell jolted at Walter's question. He had felt his mind darken, become clouded as he tried to understand what it was he was looking at. Directing the torchlight to the central mound he felt a fresh wave of revulsion as he witnessed a gruesome blob detach itself from the main bulk and fall with a nauseating splat to the wet ground. *It's alive*, he thought. *Whatever that thing is, it's alive.*

With a further disgusting squelch a thick, viscous patch at the top fell free.

"Let's get out of here." Walters was almost babbling.

Russell stood there for what seemed an eternity, feeling the horror washing over him like the wildness of an incredible storm just past. His fingers twitched painfully at his side and terror threatened to overwhelm him utterly. There was that thick stench of rottenness and decay hanging like an invisible cloud over everything; a demonic reek that could only have been fermented in the bowels of Hell itself. That something unutterably evil and depraved had been performed here was now unquestionable. The evidence was there before his very eyes. It had not been a botched robbery as he had earlier surmised but something far more sinister—a gathering of Satanists who, from the looks of things, had succeeded in calling forth *something* from somewhere else, but had paid the ultimate price in so doing. For they were clearly dead; and undoubtedly soulless.

The formless mass, which it appeared they had summoned, was now splitting. Cracks down its fluid-leaking surfaces began to widen as with dreadful squelching sounds parts of it began to form unsightly bubbles and blisters. Treacle-like gloop dripped down it.

Walters had now retreated back into the corridor. "Sergeant! Get out of there!" He screamed.

Russell was riveted to the spot, paralysed with the horror of it all.

The mound was growing taller. Having now reached the ceiling it was spreading out like a terrible vine, appendages reaching out in an almost sentient manner. The foul liquid around its base had now spread out to the nine corpses poised along the circumference of the circle. Where it touched them the liquid seeped into their clothing, blackening their dead flesh like ink on living skin.

The corpse nearest to Russell shuddered!

Russell watched as with a creaking of leathered flesh the ancient head turned to look at him. Lambent red flames danced in the hollowed out eye sockets and there was such a malevolence in that stare that he felt his heart lurch in his chest. He watched, paralysed with terror as it got to its feet. Then he heard Walters running towards him, his cries shattering the silence.

"Let's get out of here! Now! *Run!*"

Hands gripped him forcibly and began to drag him away. Trembling, Russell swung up the torch. Drops of perspiration formed on his forehead. There was a tightness in his throat and there was a mad beating where his heart ought to have been. With a yell of helpless fear, he allowed himself to be hauled out of that dreadful room. He swore savagely under his breath and backed away slowly down the corridor, where he stood panting, trying to regain his breath. He almost screamed out loud as he saw more of those living corpses get to their feet and begin shambling towards them. Some stood, shaking the dust clear.

Snaking tendrils from that monstrous abomination which had been summoned writhed along the ceiling. Like tentacles from some demonic creature they slimed their way down the walls leaving behind dreadful trails in the dust.

What happened next was truly nightmarish.

For even as the two policemen turned to flee, to get back to the front door and as far from Thurlbury Manor as they could, one of the rapacious vine-like tendrils detached itself from the ceiling and grasped Walters around an arm. The constable screamed and tried to free himself even as Russell backed away further, helpless, too frightened to intervene.

Somehow, Walters managed to pull himself away but his relief was short-lived for in the next instant two more grasping feelers latched on to him—one coiling around his left leg, the other entwining itself about his right arm. Kicking and screaming, he was raised off the ground and held firm, like a fly caught in a spider's web.

Russell's senses were rapidly running away with him. None of this could be happening. Through terror-stricken eyes he witnessed the black tentacles as they poured down from the ceiling, losing much of their solidity and becoming more like an oleaginous flow that drenched the unfortunate constable from head to foot. No longer suspended, Walters was dropped to the floor, splashing a little in the oily puddle that had now formed there.

Thunder roared along the corridor as a wave of black liquid; a revolting effluent surged forth, flowing over the unfortunate Walters and sweeping along those terrible dead things. It crashed against the far wall, splashing halfway up to the ceiling before turning direction and gushing towards Russell.

He turned and made a dash for it. Realising that the dark tide would reach the main doorway before he did, he jumped for the stairs. No sooner had he done so than the foul outpouring engulfed the hallway, flooding the room yet drawing back from the patch of diminishing sunlight that came in through the opening.

Russell climbed higher, his torchlight picking out the arms and heads of those beings he had seen earlier; the corpses now vital ingredients of this demonic soup. There was no longer any escape for him downstairs. And as he watched the blackness began to seep, drawing itself horribly up the steps.

Turning he ran towards the stretch of web that blocked his ascent and began to savagely beat at it with his torch. Thankfully, it parted quite readily and he staggered up the remaining steps onto a broad, wood-panelled landing. His heart was thumping rapidly inside his chest, threatening to explode. Something was happening here that he couldn't even begin to understand. It seemed as though thoughts were moving and pulsing inside his brain that were not his own as he felt his sanity begin to slide away from him. In his mind he could hear the slopping and squelching noises as that amorphous, semi-liquid horror, conjured from the blackest pits of Hell oozed in pursuit.

Crashing against a door, he stumbled into one of the upper floor rooms. From a quick glance it had clearly not been affected quite as badly from the initial explosion for the furniture appeared relatively untouched. To his dismay, however, he noticed that, on the outside, the windows were completely festooned, barred almost, by layers of thick web. Still, he had to get out of here. Rushing over to the window, he picked up a small stool and hurled it at the glass.

The window smashed but the stool stuck to the grey-white net-like substance that encased the outer parts of the house.

Russell cursed. He darted back to the door and peered out, dreading to see that abominable seepage ebbing its way down the corridor. For the moment all was clear, but whether in reality or in his mind, he could hear that horrible slurping sound and he knew that it was creeping inexorably closer. It might take it some time to get to the top of the stairs but it was almost as though it knew that he was trapped.

Unless there was another set of stairs leading down. He knew that in some of these large houses there was quite often a servants' staircase. A modicum of hope sparked in his brain. Leaving the room, he turned to his right and dashed further along the corridor, throwing open doors on either side of him. All led to small rooms similar to the one that he had just left.

The merest glimpse of late evening sunlight filtered in through the web-covered windows. He could see that outside it was already getting dark.

There was no alternative stairway to be found.

With a growing desperation, he wracked his mind for ideas.

Fire. Perhaps he could burn his way out. In one of the rooms he had passed he was sure he had seen a few old oil lamps resting on a mantelpiece. Backtracking, Russell dashed into the room and removed his cigarette lighter. He grabbed one of the oil lamps. Hands trembling, the torch wedged under his arm, he fidgeted with the wick and flicked his lighter. After a few seconds of getting nothing more than sparks he managed to get it going and succeeded in lighting one of the lamps. He tweaked it to increase the flame.

Smashing the window with a hurled vase, he then set about clearing much of the glass from around the edges. Stepping back, Russell raised the lamp and with a savage cry, hurled it into the mass of sticky strands outside.

Like the stool he had thrown previously, the lamp adhered to the alien substance. Russell had been expecting this. Snatching up the remaining lamp he threw it straight at the other causing both to shatter on impact. Shielding himself from the splash of flaming oil, he pulled back, his heart sinking on seeing that it had little or no effect. For the fire was extinguished almost before it had even started. The flame was snuffed out, unable to take any kind of hold on the hellish matter. If anything, the webbing had become slightly thicker as though, in some strange way, in response to this attack. He clenched his teeth in anguished frustration.

Matters were made worse when, with an awful slurping sound Russell heard the protoplasmic entity reach the top of the stairs. Running towards the room door, he glanced outside, and saw that what had been a pool of blackness, had now reshaped itself into a gelatinous mass that squeezed itself along the corridor. In the torchlight, he could see, within its semi-transparent interior, the corpses of those he had seen earlier. In one dreadful moment, he was certain that he saw Walter's ravaged face glaring out at him, his mouth working terribly. *Could it be that he was still alive—encased within that demonic jelly?*

Fiercely, Russell slammed the door shut. Grabbing a chair, he wedged it against the handle. Throwing a swift glance at the fireplace, he briefly contemplated whether or not he could possibly make use as that as an escape route but then quickly dismissed that idea. There was no way he could fit up there.

The door juddered.

Russell ran to the window and began screaming for help, his words crazed, frantic.

Behind him, the door began to bulge inwards. Around the jambs and from underneath spread that thick blackness.

Madly, Russell began to hack at the sticky strands that sealed him in. His torch quickly became enmeshed, glued and unusable. And then the door burst asunder and the horrifying bulk leaked through, threatening to engulf him, to absorb him, body and soul. Thick, dripping, tarry pseudopods reached out towards him.

Suddenly there came a powerful splash against the window and Russell was hit with a spray of water. The viscous web coating disintegrated and he could have sworn that he heard a mewling sound from the midnight-black blob as it withdrew its questing appendages.

A second gout of water siphoned into the room through the now clear window, arcing inside where some of it struck the disgusting bulk that was now pulling back. Where it hit, the thing sizzled and spat like bacon in a frying pan. Great wisps of smoke rose into the air.

"Sergeant Russell!" cried a voice from outside. "Constable Walters!"

Russell struggled to preserve his sanity. He stood watching for a moment as the shapeless jelly juddered its way out of the room, stomach-churning trails of smoking residue left in its wake. It began to liquefy.

Again came the agitated cries from outside.

Confusedly, he stumbled to the window and looked down. Below him, in the Manor grounds was a large red fire engine, its powerful hose held by two firemen and directed at him. Standing nearby was Father Barton, the senior fireman and—*Bradley Higgins!* The latter now free of the webs that had covered him.

For a time, the sergeant's mind swam, unable to comprehend any of this. And then a ladder was being winched up towards him.

"Get out of there!" Barton shouted. "For the sake of your soul, get out of there!"

With that warning given, the last rays of sunlight vanished from the sky. The headlights of the fire engine were already on, illuminating the wide-open doorway. Suddenly there was a cry and in the next instant the vile entity poured forth from the front door, its festering, corpse-saturated mass caught in the twin beams.

From his vantage point, Russell tensed as he saw the blackness spill out. It was like looking down on a befouling oil slick—one in which partially dissolved corpses bobbed and screamed. A tide of pure evil, it pulsed towards the fire engine. It was perhaps less than ten yards away when a torrent of water fired from the hose fountained forth, raining down upon it and drenching it in a deluge of holy water. For the entire vehicle and its supply of water had been blessed by Barton, who even now was shouting aloud the words of the *Pater Noster* and making the sign of the cross with a crucifix he held in his hand.

The jet of holy water burnt into the thing like a strong acid. Unsightly pieces stretched and snapped like over-tensioned rubber. Parts of it ballooned out as the dead encased within howled and struggled for release—a release they found in the purifying baptism provided by the two firemen, whose initial scepticism had turned to grim determination. Advancing as the blob retreated, they concentrated their hosing until the main essence had been utterly expunged, flushed out of existence. Later they would douse down the entire Manor to ensure it had all been removed.

Russell waited until the ladder was set in place, his mind a jumble of chaotic thoughts.

Clambering over the windowsill, he awkwardly made his way out and down the ladder.

"I'm glad to see you're alive, sergeant," the senior fireman steadied Russell as he staggered off the final rung.

Some measure of lucidity was slowly returning to Russell. He looked to Barton and then Higgins. "How?" It was the only question he could ask at that moment.

Barton stepped forward. "A few minutes after you left St. Leonard's to come here Mr. Higgins came to. I couldn't believe it, thinking as you did that he was no longer alive. He urged me to get over here, informing me that, well…" With a hand gesture he encouraged the burglar to relate the rest.

"Well…" Higgins began hesitantly. He knew full well that he was going to go to jail but right now, all things considered, that was a prospect he was almost welcoming. "I was just havin' a look about, see. Tryin' to get my hands on anythin' that might be worth a little somethin.' Next thing I hears these cars pullin' up in the drive and I thinks to myself that I'd better find some-where to hide. Luckily I managed to get in a cubbyhole under the stairs. I heard voices. Lots of them and I knew whoever these folk were they weren't the kind to mess with even though they talked posh. I overheard one of them saying that he'd padlocked the main gate which didn't matter to me for I'd come over the wall. I dunno how long I hid there. Must've been a couple of hours. At one point I heard someone scream and then there was some weird chantin.' And then…and then there came the explo-sion. The cubbyhole door was blown clear and it gashed my forehead. There was dust everywhere. I crept out and had a look in that main room. That's when I saw them bodies. I knew they were dead and I made to grab a nice-lookin' little medal-thing one was wearin' around his neck when this bloody awful thing burst out of the floor, coverin' me in God knows what. After that I legged it. Don't remember much of what came next but I felt certain I had to get to the church."

Father Barton took up the tale. "Once I'd learned what I could from Mr. Higgins and seen the effect that water from the church font had on his bindings I got Mr. Bowden to take us to the fire station, knowing only too well that you were going to need assistance here. You know my brother, Ralph, don't you?" He gestured to the senior firemen. He added slightly sententiously: "This is ample proof, if proof were needed of where dabbling in the Black Arts can lead. And what of Constable Walters? Is he still in there?"

Russell was in a daze, oblivious to the priest's questions. Blankly, he looked around him, seeing that the firemen were in the process of dousing down the smouldering jellified remains. His mind was reeling now that he was no longer in a survival situation, the utter mind-shattering reality of what he had just experienced taking a firmer hold on his crumbling sanity. He was aware that more questions were being asked of him but shock was now overtaking him. His last image before he collapsed was of that terrible, slimy, corpse-strewn patch on the drive of Thurlbury Manor.

ABOUT THE AUTHOR

As penance for past deeds, Edmund Glasby grew up in More-cambe and studied Egyptian Archaeology at University College London and Archaeology and Anthropology at Oxford—More-cambe, which has more than its share of the strange and unsavoury, provided him with a better education. After turning his back on academia, he now writes in the genres of dark fantasy and supernatural thriller, having been brought up on horror; his father was John S. Glasby the prolific supernatural writer.

2010 saw the publication of his first novel, *Disciple of a Dark God,* a far-ranging dark fantasy epic. His first collection of supernatural stories, *The Dyrsgol Horror and Others* was published by Borgo in 20013, and was followed by *The Ash Murders*, *The Chaos of Chung-Fu*, *Ghouls of the Undercity*, *Labyrinth of the Lost*, and *Dark Shadows*. Currently he is working on two detective novels.

When he is not writing, he is the captain of a local archery club and he has won a trophy or two both at local and European level with the English longbow he made.